# THE SHAKEOUT

As their lips met, a small part of his mind heard a small click. It was so faint as to be almost inaudible. It could have been a spoon shifting in a saucer, or the mattress yielding to new pressures. Piers reacted instinctively.

He jerked away from Anne like a twanged bowstring, every taut muscle moving in a co-ordinated swing. He dropped on all fours to get out of the line of fire and crossed the floor to the open window in a blurred forward roll. As he came off the floor and reached for the window-sill a shadow moved on the verandah outside. Piers vaulted the sill and landed with his back to the railings.

He struck out at the shadow, landing four piston punches in a second. Then he grabbed the man's clothing and pushed him backwards through the window into the bedroom. He jumped through afterwards, landing with his knee in the man's belly.

It was the painter he had seen working on the railings. A small camera was attached to his wrist.

Somebody wanted pictures of Piers Roper and Anne Mainwaring in bed together.

# The Shakeout

# Ken Follett

**CORONET BOOKS**
Hodder and Stoughton

*Author's Acknowledgement*
I thank Sue Baker, the Motoring correspondent
of the London *Evening News,* for her advice.


Copyright © 1975 by Ken Follett

First published in Great Britain 1975 by
Harwood-Smart Publishing Company Limited

*Coronet edition 1976*
*Fourth impression 1982*

---

Printed and bound in Great Britain for
Hodder and Stoughton Paperbacks, a
division of Hodder and Stoughton Ltd.,
Mill Road, Dunton Green, Sevenoaks, Kent
(Editorial Office : 47 Bedford Square,
London, WC1 3DP) by Richard Clay
(The Chaucer Press), Ltd., Bungay, Suffolk

ISBN 0 340 21018 4

# One

The waiter brought a fillet steak, covered in some kind of thick sauce, on a plate which was much too large for the food it had to hold. Piers Roper ignored it and sipped his claret.

Andrew Cliss turned to his wife, Elisabeth, and said in a light tone: "Ordering steak in an Italian restaurant is all part of Piers' image, you know. In Claridge's he asks for a hamburger, in Lee Kwuk Ho's he wants Wiener Schnitzel."

Elisabeth's brown eyes looked steadily at Roper. "I think he just eats what he wants."

Roper refused to acknowledge the innuendo in Elisabeth's words. Andrew had not seen the look she had given Piers. Piers was glad: there were limits to using old friends, and their wives were outside those limits. He smiled at Andrew and adopted the same bantering tone. "You chose the restaurant," he said.

"So I did. Do you like it?"

Roper looked around. In truth he did not like it. The tiled floor, hard wooden chairs, and marble-topped tables were too deliberate an attempt to create an image. The place was supposed to be typically Italian: in Italy it would look like a lorry-drivers' pull-in.

"I'll let you know when I've tasted the food," he replied evasively, and Andrew smiled. Piers had been slowly drinking wine while his companions ploughed their way through soup and some sea food concoction. They had a bottle of Bollinger between them, and Piers was trying not to drink faster than the two of them put together.

Another waiter arrived with baby marrows on a stainless

steel dish, and delicately shovelled them on to Piers' plate. When he went Piers sliced into the steak and watched the juices from its rare centre swirl and darken in the gravy, like streaks of oil in a rain puddle.

When he had chewed and swallowed, Andrew looked at him inquiringly.

"I like the restaurant," Piers said.

"Good." Andrew insisted on playing the role of host, even though it had been Piers who had rung up and arranged the evening, and paid for the box at the opera.

Cliss spoke to his wife again. "You see this respectable, successful middle-aged executive here. I remember him running a lady's corset up the flagpole at one of England's most distinguished colleges."

Elisabeth laughed. Piers said: "It was a long time ago, Elisabeth."

"But I don't think you've grown up as much as you pretend," she replied.

Piers let the comment ride. Andrew had always maintained his own picture of Roper as an adventure-seeking youth. He had no idea of the truth, but you couldn't completely fool an old friend. Or his wife, it seemed.

That had a lot to do with the choice of restaurant, Piers suspected. It was full of beautiful young people, one or two with vaguely familiar faces. No doubt it was the in place at the moment. Andrew would think Piers felt at home among them. On the contrary, he considered that at the age of forty-one he was entitled to ignore youth and eat with his own generation.

The dessert trolley was rolled over to their table. Andrew and Elisabeth chose large portions of extravagant gateaux with cream poured all over them. Piers asked for black coffee and blue Stilton, and ordered three large brandies.

Andrew rolled his eyes at the first mouthful of his sweet. "Piers, you don't know what you're missing," he said.

"That's why he's that shape and you're this shape," Elisa-

6

beth said, patting her husband's waistcoat.

Piers finished the last of his claret. "If you want to stay healthy, you have to choose between booze and good food some time in your late twenties," he said. "I chose booze."

"I suspect you faced another choice in your twenties, Piers," said Elisabeth.

He smiled mockingly at her, challenging her to read his mind. "Go on."

"I think you chose work instead of love."

"No, that just sort of happened."

Andrew cut in: "He chose play instead of love, if you ask me. Hey, listen, I'm the one supposed to take the mickey out of Piers."

Roper looked at the man opposite him, taking in the strained waistcoat buttons, the muttonchop whiskers which had lately come back into fashion, the large ring on the fleshy finger. He noted the slightly clumsy way Andrew had smoothed over a rather-too-personal remark of his wife's. And he thought: You and I are so far apart, now, Andrew.

Suddenly Cliss said: "Anyhow, how is work?"

Piers collected his thoughts quickly. "It's going too well," he said.

"Too well?" Andrew looked puzzled.

"You know me, Andrew," Piers said. "I get restless."

"True," Andrew said. He turned to Elisabeth. "I've never known you stay in one job for more than ... what: five years?"

"Three," Piers said. "And I've been with International Business Computers for two. I'd like to market something else. Engineering, maybe."

"Hm." Andrew looked thoughtful.

Piers decided to change the subject. "Are we going to have some more brandy here, or will you two come to my flat and help me wave goodbye to a bottle?"

"Neither, but thanks," Andrew said. "If I get drunk to-night, tomorrow will be hell." He raised a hand and a waiter materialised. "The bill," he said.

"This has been marvellous," Piers said. "I'd like to do it again."

Elisabeth said: "I'm sure you two prefer your more usual pub crawls, with no ladies allowed."

"Usual!" Andrew pretended to be outraged. "About once every five years we meet and get paralytic together and you call that our usual pub crawl."

"Whatever it is, I think you prefer it to be all male."

They stood up. Andrew left five five-pound notes on the table. They walked to the door where a waiter got their coats.

"Besides," Andrew said, continuing the conversation, "you're mistaken if you think Piers isn't fond of female company. I have quite a job keeping our pub crawls all-male." He helped his wife on with her coat. "Remind me to tell you about Piers and his ladies some time," he added.

Roper wondered why he was going on about it. Perhaps that look Elisabeth had given Piers had not escaped Andrew after all.

Outside, he shook hands with the couple and insisted they take the first cab. "Au revoir," he said. "Thank you for a very good meal."

Andrew ushered Elisabeth into the cab. "Thank you for a good opera," he said.

The taxi drove away and another immediately pulled up, but Roper turned away from it. The time was eleven-thirty, and he was almost sober. He walked south, away from the restaurant and towards Oxford Street.

He saw a phone box, made a decision, and went in. He dialled a number from memory, then pushed a coin into the slot. He said: "This is Roper. Have someone come to my flat in half an hour, would you?" Then he hung up.

He pulled his scarf close about his throat as he walked on, looking out for a cab. The thin white silk gave little protection against the cold May wind rushing between high buildings on both sides of the street.

He reached Oxford Street and stood at the kerb. There were scores of taxis, all occupied. He wished now he had taken the one at the restaurant, and phoned from home.

He saw a yellow "For Hire" light a hundred yards away towards Tottenham Court Road. He watched it approach him, then suddenly pull in to the kerb. The light went off and a couple got in. "Damn," he said under his breath.

When a free cab finally came along he almost missed it. His shout could not be heard in the roar of the midnight traffic, and he could not whistle. He had to jump into the road almost in front of the vehicle to stop it.

"Get yourself killed that way, mate," the driver said. Roper gave the man his address and got in. Cabbies never called you Guv any more, he thought. Perhaps they were not so dependent upon tips as in the old days. More likely, they had decided that being subservient was not the best approach. If the driver treated you as an equal, you had to give him a hefty tip to prove your superiority. That's called marketing, Roper thought, allowing himself a private smile in the darkness of the cab.

The car turned left at Marble Arch and went down Park Lane: a twelve-lane highway now, Roper reflected, and still it gets jammed up. The motor industry and the road building lobby made sure sanity did not prevail. That's marketing, he thought again.

The taxi speeded up along Grosvenor Place, past the back of Buckingham Palace, and turned right into Belgravia, the Diplomatic Ghetto. Roper yawned, and wondered whether he was as sober as he had thought. The Wagner was ringing in his ears.

He gave the cabbie a pound and walked away without waiting for change, thus proving his own theory. He climbed a flight of stairs and let himself into his flat.

The comfortable, old-fashioned furniture relaxed him, as it was meant to. He hung his coat in the cloakroom and crossed

9

the hall to the drawing-room. As the music was playing in his head, he decided he might as well listen to the real thing. He found a record of the opera and put it on the Bang & Olufsen.

He poured brandy into a glass and took off his tie. He sipped the brandy neat, then remembered the phone call he had made and prudently squirted soda into the goblet.

He took a Senior Service from the box on the table, lit it, inhaled, then sat back. Tobacco, brandy, Wagner, and a good day's work done. He had planted a seed tonight. He did not know when it would poke its shoot above the earth, but he was comfortably sure that it would.

The doorbell interrupted his thoughts, sounding a mongrel note fractionally below top A which soured the music from the hi-fi. Roper had asked the electrician who had installed the bell whether it could be tuned. The man had looked at him as if he were a crackpot, he remembered as he opened the front door.

He looked with approval at the girl who walked in. She had shoulder-length hair, a rich colour between brown and red. The tailored coat she wore was a tasteful autumn shade which blended well with her natural colouring, and reached just below the tops of her boots. When Roper greeted her she smiled pleasantly and said: "How do you do."

He pointed to the cloakroom and said: "If you'd like to put your coat in there." She turned. "Oh," he said. He pulled a drawer under the telephone table and took out an envelope. "Let me give you this now."

"Thank you," she said, and went into the cloakroom.

He waited for her in the drawing-room. When she came, his first impression of her was confirmed. She was very beautiful. "Would you like a drink?" he offered.

"Please. Vodka, tonic, ice," she said crisply. She looked at the paintings on the walls.

He made her drink and took it to her. He kissed her lips, once, softly. "I think you're very beautiful," he said.

"Thank you," she said, taking the drink. "But then, you have old-fashioned tastes, Piers."

He smiled. "I'm rather old."

She touched his arm. "But thin, hard, and not a little attractive. I'm going to enjoy this."

He wondered whether to believe her, and decided it did not matter. He took her hand. "Bring your drink," he said.

He led her into the hall and through to the bedroom.

He set his glass down beside the bed, drew back the sheet, and quickly slipped out of his clothes. He lay on the bed, his drink in one hand, supporting himself with the other elbow, and watched the girl.

She was neither coy nor exhibitionist about her body. She undid the row of buttons down the front of her dress slowly, then took off her shoes and tights. Her skin was slightly tanned, and Roper thought how difficult that must have been, with her colouring.

He savoured the sight of her, as he might have tasted a good wine. She reached behind her back to unfasten her brassiere. Her superb breasts spilled out of the garment, and Roper pulled her to him and buried his face in the soft, simple warmth of her.

The seed Roper sowed in the restaurant that evening sprouted six months later.

He sat in his office, high above the wet pavements of St. Paul's Churchyard, reading The Financial Times. The report in the newspaper, ostensibly a review of recent developments in computer technology, was in fact an informative plug for IBC's new software range. Roper's press officer, Alex Cole, had done a good job.

He turned the page, and a single paragraph near the foot of a column caught his eye. It read: "The Senior Marketing Executive of the Holmes Motor Corporation, Mr. Isaac Davis, has resigned because of ill-health, it was announced yesterday."

The time of patient waiting was over. Now Roper had to move in fast.

He took his book of telephone numbers out of the top drawer of the desk and looked up Andrew Cliss. He picked up the grey phone, a private line which did not pass through the office switchboard, and dialled the number. As it rang out he scribbled on his desk pad: "Restaurant reminder—shooting—mention Dean—mention Davis—mention IBC."

A voice said: "Cliss Components, can I help you?"

"Andrew Cliss," said Roper.

"Putting you through." There was a pause, then a different woman's voice said: "Mr. Cliss' office."

"This is Piers Roper."

"I'm sorry, Mr. Roper, but Mr. Cliss is not here today. Can I take a message?"

"No thank you." Roper pressed the handset cradle and got a dialling tone again, then rang Andrew's home. He was relieved to hear Andrew's voice answer.

"Piers here, Andrew. How are you?"

"Fine, Piers. What can I do you for?"

"The restaurant we went to a few months ago. I want to take someone there and I've forgotten the name." As he said this, Roper crossed out the words "Restaurant reminder" on his pad.

Andrew laughed. "Now it's funny you should say that, Piers. Elisabeth and I had an argument about that night—she said you hated the restaurant and I said you liked it."

Elisabeth is more perceptive than you, old friend, Roper thought. He said: "Looks like you won the argument."

"Yes. Anyway, it's the Trattoria Vitrone."

"Thank you. We'll go there again some time. Did you go shooting this year?" Roper drew another line on his pad.

"Yes, with Lord Ashton. A marvellous shoot. Laurence Dean was there. Do you know him?"

"No." On his pad Roper crossed out the words "Mention

Dean". Cliss had made things easier by mentioning the name himself. Piers was not surprised. The fact that Andrew knew Laurence Dean quite well was the reason for the meeting in the restaurant six months ago.

Roper went on: "I see Dean has just lost a good senior executive."

"Oh?"

"Isaac Davies. Know him?"

"Of course! I do a great deal of business with Holmes. But I didn't know about Davis."

Roper crossed another item off his list. "How is Cliss Components, these days."

"Always in profit, always in debt. How about International Business Computers? Are you still with them?"

"Afraid so. Listen, Andrew, I must go. Good to hear your voice."

"Hold on, Piers, I've just had—" Roper cut him off before he could finish the sentence.

He pressed a key on the intercom and leaned forward to speak to his secretary. "Get me Alex Cole," he said. A minute later the blue phone purred.

"I read the article in The Financial Times, Alex," Roper said. "Well done."

"Thank you, Piers."

"Listen. I want to meet Laurence Dean, the Managing Director of the Holmes Motor Corporation. Now they have a new car coming out quite soon, I think. I want you to find out the date, time and place of the launch—Dean is sure to be there. Get on to the PR for the company and get me invited. Also arrange for me to be introduced to Dean."

"I'll get on to that now," Cole replied. Roper hung up. He sat at his desk for a moment, looking at the telephone, then he got up. He took his black, single-breasted overcoat from its hanger inside a cupboard by the door, and put it on. Then he fixed his bowler hat firmly on his head, glanced in the mirror on the inside of the cupboard door, and went out.

"Ten minutes, Miss Roberts," he said to his elderly secretary as he passed her desk. She made a note on her pad. Roper went down to the ground floor in the elevator and walked quickly through the lobby into the street.

The wind howled between the high buildings as he strode along the pavement. I wonder whether the architects who build these concrete canyons realise that they are wind tunnels, he thought.

He crossed the road to a tobacconist's shop and bought twenty Senior Service. "Would you let me have some two-penny coins in the change, for the telephone?" he asked the assistant.

"Sorry, we're short of change," she replied.

He would have to use a ten-penny coin, thereby increasing the Post Office's profit on his phone call by a factor of about ten. How many people paid over the odds for their phone calls simply because they did not have change? Abolishing the shilling slot had been a good marketing move.

Piers, you're becoming cynical, he thought. He left the shop and walked around a corner, out of sight of his office, to a telephone kiosk. He lit a cigarette before dialling.

The phone was answered quickly. The voice said "Palmer."

"Roper. I'm arranging to meet Dean soon. I want to be able to impress him in a short time." He paused. "The company must by now have done some preliminary thinking about in-board computers for its cars. Do we know, or can we find out, what they have decided?"

"Wait while I see whether we know," Palmer said. Roper drew on his cigarette and looked through the windows of the kiosk. He saw a secretary from IBC walking towards the box, and turned away so that she would not see his face. Even a young secretary might wonder why one of the firm's top executives needed to make a call from a phone box; and Roper did not like people to wonder.

14

Palmer's voice came on the line again. "They did an exercise a few months back," he said.. "We have the report. What do you want to know?"

"The size of machine they think they need. Where in the car it is located. Briefly, the operations it will carry out."

"Size: a quarter of a cubic foot. Location: behind the dashboard. Functions: control of fuel mix, monitoring of reservoirs in hydraulic systems, also electrics."

"Thank you," said Roper, and hung up. He left the kiosk and walked quickly back to the office.

As he went in, Miss Roberts looked over her tortoise-shell glasses and said: "Mr. Cole left you a message. It's on your desk."

Roper hung up his hat and coat and crossed the room to his desk. The message read: "All fixed. Thursday next, twelve noon, Grafton Hotel."

Roper sat down and gave a sigh of satisfaction. It was all falling into place very nicely.

The company Rolls eased to a halt outside the Grafton Hotel, and a uniformed flunkey raced the chauffeur to the car door. The flunkey won, and Roper got out. Alex Cole told the chauffeur to return to the office, tipped the flunkey, and followed Roper through the automatic doors of the tall building.

Roper looked around the lobby with mild distaste. It was not quite a top hotel, and the bits of slightly worn red velvet and gilt paintwork made it look like the foyer of a theatre. He presumed Britain's third largest car manufacturers had their reasons for choosing the place.

His eye lighted on a signboard which said, in white letters pegged into holes in the black plastic: "Holmes Motor Corporation—Viennese Suite."

Cole caught up with him and pointed a finger. "It's over here," he said.

A dolly bird wearing rimless spectacles welcomed them at the entrance to the suite. Cole gave their names, and she handed each of them a stiff paper folder. It was pale green—the colour which identified the company—and bore the words "Press Kit".

In the centre of the big room, on a circular dais, was what Roper presumed to be the new car. It was wrapped in pale green paper and tied at the top with a huge bow, like a Christmas present. Roper sat down at a table near the back of the room.

"Drink?" Alex asked.

"Please." Roper waited, to see whether Cole knew what his boss drank.

Cole said: "Let me see—Johnnie Walker, fifty-fifty, no ice."

Roper nodded, and Cole went to the bar. Piers looked around the room. On the far side television crews were making last-minute adjustments and testing lights. Still photographers sat at tables on one side of the dais, and around Piers' place were the motoring writers.

He presumed that leading car dealers were being intro-duced to the new car at similar parties all over the country. He opened his green folder, and saw the programme for the afternoon. He hoped to leave well before that got under way.

So far he was not impressed with Holmes' marketing set-up. The hotel was wrong, the idea of wrapping the car up with a ribbon was old hat, and the whole thing was starting too late in the day. By the time the assembled media men had looked at the car, eaten a heavy lunch, and been driven out to the test track at Wembley, the light would be fading.

Cole returned with the drinks and sat down. He leafed through the papers in the folder. Roper sipped his whisky.

"What do you think of it?" Piers asked.

"This?" said Alex, lifting the folder. "It's all there—pictures, diagrams, specifications, options, lots of blurb, performance figures, variations, colour schemes. It's a competent, uninspired press kit."

"Just like the whole do," Roper said, half to himself. Competent but uninspired. Holmes definitely needed a new senior marketing man.

A small group of men entered by a door Roper had not noticed. There were five of them, but the group seemed to be dominated by a shortish, stout man of about fifty-five. Another of the men walked across to a microphone on a stand beside the dais. He cleared his throat, and the burble of voices in the room died to a low murmur.

He said: "Gentlemen, welcome. May I introduce the Managing Director of the Holmes Motor Corporation, Mr. Laurence Dean."

There was scattered applause which faded quickly. The stout man Roper had noticed came over to the microphone.

"I'm here to introduce you to the Holmes Capricorn," he said. Roper tuned out the words and studied the man. His deep voice, frayed at the edges by a lifetime of smoking, retained a trace of Midlands accent in the vowels. The sandy hair was thin on top and cropped unfashionably close at the sides and back, emphasising the round, lined face. Put him in a sheepskin coat and a trilby, and he would look like a farmer, Roper thought. His cheeks even had the redness of weather-damaged blood vessels, although in his case the damage was more likely caused by malt whisky.

But Dean was not wearing a sheepskin coat. In fact he had a blue-black pinstripe suit, similar to Roper's except that Roper's fitted better. There the sartorial resemblance ended. Dean's shirt was light blue, with a club tie, and cuff-links glinted at his wrists. Roper wore a white shirt and plain black knitted tie, and his cuffs buttoned. He hated ostentation.

Dean's shoes were of a kind Roper would never have worn: they had elastic gussets at the sides instead of laces. Roper wore laced Church's brogues. The subtle, but definite difference

17

in style between the two men would do no harm, Piers decided. Nobody hired his double—the employee was too likely to end up firing the employer.

Dean's speech ended. He climbed on to the dais and took hold of one end of the bow. When he pulled, the wrapping fell away neatly and revealed the new car. There was a round of applause, lengthy and enthusiastic this time.

Roper clapped mechanically. He was unimpressed by the car. It had the blunt rear end which had been pioneered by one of Holmes' competitors a year ago; twin headlights which were old hat; and an unsightly ridge in the bonnet which would undoubtedly be called a power bulge.

Cameras rolled and flashguns clicked. A flock of half-dressed girls appeared from nowhere and decorated the dais, opening doors, sitting in the car, lifting the boot lid and winding the windows. Roper waited patiently.

Soon the girls receded and the pressmen descended on the car. Roper gave them a few minutes. Dean had retreated to the side of the room, and was engaging in short conversations with a series of people.

"All right," Roper said finally to Alex Cole. "Let's go." Cole got up and crossed the room to a man standing near Dean. A few words passed between them, then Cole looked at Roper and nodded.

Piers got up and went over to his press officer. Cole introduced the man he was with as Holmes' Chief Public Relations Officer. The man turned and caught Dean's sleeve.

"Larry, I want you to meet Piers Roper. He's from IBC."

Dean extended his hand and gave the mechanical smile which comes from being introduced to too many people. Then the skin around his eyes wrinkled and the smile became genuine.

"Mr. Roper," he said. "I knew your father."

Piers was not surprised: Many businessmen of Dean's generation had met Allen Roper.

Dean continued: "A very sad loss. Eight years, now, isn't it?"

"Six," Roper corrected.

"Yes. Do you keep up that marvellous house in Dorset?"

"No," Piers said. "I'm afraid the Inland Revenue took that." In fact the estate and the mansion had been sold to pay his father's creditors, who had been numerous. Allen Roper's business success had not matched his social popularity.

Piers moved slightly, so that Dean had to turn a fraction in order to avoid being impolite. The movement cut the two PR men out of the conversation, and the backs of Roper and Dean would insulate them from interruption for a few minutes.

"Congratulations on the Capricorn," Piers said. "It's a fine car."

"Thank you."

"Cars are getting much more sophisticated, mechanically," Piers continued.

"Of course," Dean agreed. He looked past Roper, betraying the beginnings of impatience.

"By now you must be thinking about inboard computers."

Dean's attention switched back to Roper with an almost visible jerk. A little smile touched the corners of his mouth as he saw the drift of the conversation. He said: "I don't suppose I'm giving any secrets away if I admit that."

"We're thinking about them at IBC," Piers went on. "My guess is you'll want something about the size of a shoe box, to fit behind the dash. It will control fuel mix, monitor hydraulic systems, and provide primary electrical diagnosis."

Dean smiled fully now, and opened his mouth to speak. Piers interrupted him. "I don't want to prise information out of you," he said, matching Dean's smile. "I just want you to know that when you're ready, IBC will be able to match your specifications." He put out his hand. "It's been a pleasure talking to you, sir," he said. He turned away and spoke to Alex Cole. The Holmes PR stepped to Dean's side.

Roper and Cole walked back to the bar. Piers was wondering about that final "sir". He had put it in to offset the aggressiveness of his exhortation, but on reflection he thought it too salesmanlike.

The bartender poured him a generous Scotch, and he drank half of it in one swallow.

"Work out well?" Alex inquired.

"Fine," Piers said. "Thank you for fixing it." He emptied his glass and pushed it across the bar for a refill.

Roper picked up The Times from the table in the centre of the smoking-room at his club. En route to his seat, he stopped a waiter and said: "Would you get me a drink, Brown?"

"Certainly, Mr. Roper," the man replied.

Piers settled into a comfortable leather seat, nodding to a couple of acquaintances nearby.

He looked about him as he waited for his drink. He had not wanted to join the club at first, fifteen years ago, when Palmer had proposed him. Now he could hardly imagine life without it. The club had once had something to do with motoring, but now only the veteran cars whose pictures hung on the panelled walls survived to remind members. Most of them, like Roper, used it simply as a convenient place to eat and drink in the company of their own kind.

The waiter brought his whisky, mixed exactly right. He sipped it, set it down beside him on an occasional table placed there for that purpose, and folded the paper in four. He took out his pen and looked at the crossword in the bottom left-hand corner of the back page.

He did not see the man sit down beside him, because he was engrossed in 22 down: "Creature's extremity at point of small piece." It had four letters. "Point" almost certainly referred to the compass points, so was one of the letters N, S, E, or W. He wondered whether "piece" meant a weapon of some kind.

"Tough one, Piers?" said the man next to him.

Roper looked up and saw Andrew Cliss. He smiled. "I have it now," he said. He filled in "pawn" for 22 down, then dropped the newspaper on his lap and put his pen in his inside jacket pocket.

"I was hoping I'd run into you here," Cliss went on. "Not disturbing you, am I?"

"It's a pleasure to see you, Andrew." The waiter hovered, and Roper said: "Drink?"

"No, thanks. Elisabeth is expecting me."

"Why did you want to run into me?"

"Well." Andrew lowered his voice quite unnecessarily and leaned forward. "I saw Larry Dean today. I think you know he's looking for a new Head of Marketing."

Roper nodded.

"Well, I remembered that you had said you wanted a move, and mentioned engineering. I took the liberty of mentioning your name to Larry."

"Oh," said Roper flatly. He was secretly amused that Cliss thought the whole thing was his own idea.

"I hope you don't mind," Andrew said.

"Not at all. Good of you to think of me. It's just that I hadn't thought about the motor industry."

"Oh," said Cliss, sounding disappointed. "The thing is, Larry was rather keen. Apparently the two of you met only a couple of days ago."

"That's right."

"He liked you, it seems. I don't know how long you talked with him, but you managed to give the impression of being an effective, imaginative executive with some knowledge of the car business."

"Good Lord," Roper said.

"I rather thought Holmes might fit the bill for you."

"So it might," Roper said, pretending to consider the idea for the first time. He sipped his drink reflectively.

"Anyway, old chap, not to put too fine a point on it, Larry

21

asked me to put out feelers."

Roper put his drink down again. "Then you can let him know I'm interested," he said, with the air of one who suddenly makes up his mind.

"Marvellous," Andrew said. "Well, I mustn't let Elisabeth get cross."

Roper stood up. "I'm very grateful to you for this, Andrew," he said.

"Don't mention it. That's what old friends are for. Goodbye, Piers."

"Goodbye," Piers said. He sat down again and picked up the crossword. Yes, he thought, that's what old friends are for.

The seed finally bore fruit a week later.

The green phone on Roper's desk hummed softly. When he picked it up his secretary said: "Mr. Laurence Dean is calling you, Mr. Roper."

Piers smiled. In a week Holmes Motors had done a thorough research job on him, and they now had a dossier with complete details of his education, career to date, performance in his present job, and character assessments from a dozen former colleagues.

"Put him on," he said.

Roper's secretary said: "Mr. Roper is on the line."

At the other end another secretary said: "Thank you. Mr. Roper, I have Mr. Dean for you." There was a pause. "Mr. Dean, Mr. Roper is on the line."

Dean said: "Good morning Roper."

"How are you, Mr. Dean."

"I enjoyed talking to you the other day, Roper, but we didn't have much time. I'd like to meet with you again."

"I'd like that."

"Good. Well now look. I'm spending a weekend in Essex shortly, with one or two people from Holmes. How about coming down? It'll be the weekend of the 20th."

Roper paused. You have done well, Piers, he thought. "That's fine. I look forward to it."

"Splendid. I'll get my secretary to let you have the address and so on. Come down on the Saturday morning."

"Thank you."

"Splendid. Goodbye now."

Roper hung up. Dean had not said anything about a wife, which meant he had read the dossier on Roper well enough to know he was a bachelor. The fact that it was a weekend invitation meant two things: Dean was pretty keen on Roper, and the company as a whole was more concerned than usual about who was going to head up its marketing operation. Piers was not the only one to have noted their slackness.

He would be on show for inspection by most of the company's top executives. What was more, his invitation was for Saturday and Sunday. The rest of them would be briefed on Roper's background on Friday night.

He ran over the conversation again and decided there was nothing else to be learned from it. He leaned back in his chair, took a cigarette from the packet beside the phone, and lit it.

His mouth curled in a rare, tigerish smile, giving his features a predatory look which few people were privileged to witness. "I'll eat 'em up alive," he said aloud.

# Two

As soon as the snow fell, London dirtied it. Roper looked with distaste at the muddy slush on the pavement as he walked briskly down Ludgate Hill. The white flakes had looked attractive as they meandered past his twelfth-floor office window, blissfully ignorant of the mucky fate that awaited them underneath the shoes of City commuters. About half an inch had fallen, then the weather had given up in disgust.

Roper turned left at Ludgate Circus and crossed the Thames by Blackfriars Bridge. He was looking out for a call-box. He did not like to use the same phone twice when contacting Palmer. Of course, that was no safeguard against a wiretap at Palmer's end; but that was unlikely. Palmer was as obsessively cautious as Roper. And if Palmer's phone were tapped, that would be the end of it all anyway.

He found a kiosk on the Southwark side of the river and went in. As usual, his ring was answered immediately.

"Palmer."

"Roper here. It looks as if I will get the job with Holmes. I'm to spend a weekend with Dean and his top brass."

"Good. I must brief you more fully now. We had better meet."

"If you say so."

"Is Saturday clear?"

"Yes."

"Keep it free. I'll be in touch." Palmer rang off.

Roper left the phone box and hailed a taxi. He gave his home address. The cabbie drove along the south side of the river, past Waterloo and Lambeth Palace, then crossed

Lambeth Bridge and went up through Victoria, thus avoiding Parliament Square. The man had long hair and a droopy moustache, and wore jeans. Roper wondered whether the old breed of London taxi-drivers was dying out. When the hippie cabbie asked him the way from Victoria, Roper decided it was.

When he got home, Roper left his wet shoes and heavy overcoat in the cloakroom and went into the bedroom to change. He sat on the bed for a moment, thinking about what to do with the evening. He felt quite free to go anywhere—Palmer's message would find him whether he was in the West End or Notting Hill. Not that Roper was ever in Notting Hill.

But he knew he would not enjoy a play, or a meal in a restaurant, because of the tension of a meeting with Palmer. He decided to spend the evening at home.

He undressed to his black, stretch nylon underpants—one of the few concessions he made to fashion. In fact, it had nothing to do with fashion: he had never liked the long white underwear shorts men had worn in the fifties.

Just off his bedroom was a small room which had been designed as a dressing-room. Roper had installed block floors and some expensive equipment and made it a gymnasium. He put on a dressing-gown and went in there.

He picked up two small dumbell weights, one in each hand, and lifted them above his head in turn, working faster and faster, until he began to perspire. Then he took off his dressing-gown, tossed it into a corner, and set to. He did a dozen knee-bends with the large dumbell, then a hundred fast skips. He pulled a bar out from the wall and adjusted it to the right level—about two feet above his head—then chinned himself a dozen times.

Into the middle of the small room he pulled a punchball with a fast spring. He hit it with left and right fists in turn, harder and harder, until his arms ached. Then he forced himself to hit the punchbag with all his might ten times with each fist. Finally he picked up the small weights and, with them in his fists, attacked the bobbing punchball again.

When he had finished his body streamed with sweat. He put on the dressing-gown again, and walked through his bedroom to the bathroom. He towelled himself all over, then stood under the shower and washed.

His body tingled pleasantly as he dressed in black slacks, a white shirt, and black leather carpet slippers. It gave him great satisfaction to know that he could still manage the exercise routine he had devised for himself ten years ago.

He went into the kitchen and opened the refrigerator. He selected a lamb chop, noting with disapproval that it was packed in a polystyrene container and sealed with some kind of cellophane. Roper disliked polystyrene: it was practically indestructible, and if people continued to use it for packaging the country would soon be snowed under with the stuff. Already he kept seeing the little white plastic globules blowing about in gutters.

He unwrapped the chop, slapped a piece of butter on top of it, and slid it under the grill. He went back to the refrigerator and found a bag of tomatoes. He took out six, throwing away any which were not perfectly firm, and sliced them on the chopping board. Then he put them under the grill.

He set a place for himself at the pine kitchen-table. His dining-room was only used when he entertained guests, which was rarely. That was a pity, because one or two of his favourite paintings were hung in the dining-room.

He drew a small glass of water from the tap above the stainless steel sink unit. Water was an underrated drink, in his opinion. He looked at his watch and decided the meal was cooked. He put the chop and the tomatoes on a china plate, sprinkled pepper liberally on the tomatoes, and sat down to eat.

He finished the meal with a small piece of cheese, and went into the drawing-room. He felt like a whisky, but decided to let his food digest first. He opened the record cabinet, selected a disc, and put in on the turntable. As Mahler's chords crashed out of the speakers, he lit a cigarette and opened a book of chess problems.

He found himself unable to solve the problem in his head, and blamed that on the tension which remained at the pit of his stomach. He crossed the room to a glass-topped chess-table under the window, and arranged the problem on the board.

During a pause in the music, he heard a soft noise in the hall. He got to his feet and padded across the carpet to the connecting door which led to the dining-room. From there, there was another connecting door to the kitchen—and from the kitchen door he could see straight down the hall.

He had left the kitchen door shut. He opened it quietly and looked out. The hall was empty. Then he saw the white envelope which lay on the mat before the front door.

He picked it up, noted that there was no name or address on the front, and slit it open. He knew by the way the sheet of paper inside was folded, that the message came from Palmer. A series of numbers was all that was typed on the paper. Roper recognised the numbers as a coded map reference, followed by a time.

He deciphered the numbers with the aid of a logarithm table, then consulted a map.

He was to meet Palmer on a beach on the South Wales coast at 12 noon on Saturday.

He crumpled the envelope and paper in his hand as he went back into the drawing-room. He put both in a big ashtray, picked up a lighter from the table, and set fire to the twisted ball. He watched the crisp white paper turn into fragile black ash. Then he went into the bathroom.

He took a sleeping pill from a bottle above the pedestal, and swallowed it without water. He went into his bedroom, undress, donned pyjamas and got into bed.

He dropped off to sleep with a feeling of dissatisfaction

27

nagging at the back of his mind. It did not occur to him to think that he was lonely.

Roper sensed the girl watching him. In the split-second before he opened his eyes, he noticed that his bedside clock-radio had switched itself on although it was Saturday; remembered sending for the call-girl late the previous night; and recalled that today he was to meet Palmer.

Then he looked at her.

Her long, straight blonde hair seemed unaffected by a night in his bed. She had propped herself up on one elbow beside him, and was studying his face. He remembered why he had sent for her: after two restless evenings at home he had been determined to break the pattern.

Her hand under the duvet rested lightly on the hard muscles of his stomach. She leaned forward and kissed his chin, and her breasts brushed his upper arm. He kissed her mouth, reached around her, and stroked the length of her tanned back and the curve of her buttocks.

Presently she rolled on top of him, and he slid inside her. She put her weight on her elbows, her perfect breasts swaying above his ribs. He took them in his hands and gently squeezed, his thumbs stroking the puckered nipples.

She pressed harder against him, and he tensed his stomach against her pelvic bone. Her eyes closed, her face became flushed, and she took her weight off her arms and lay on his chest.

She seemed to be gasping for air as she built to her climax. Roper's body was like a steel spring, tirelessly lifting and falling. Her lips curled in a snarl, and finally she gave a series of high-pitched animal cries, her back arched impossibly in an ecstatic convulsion, and she collapsed.

When her breathing eased she said: "You didn't come, did you."

"It's the time of day," Piers replied. "In the morning I'm

28

always capable but I never really make it."

She giggled. "I ought to pay you, now."

"Nonsense. It did my ego the world of good."

She rolled off and lay beside him, her blonde head in the crook of his arm. He looked down at the wide blue eyes in the flushed face, and said: "You look very pretty right now."

She snuggled up to him, and rubbed her soft cheek against his morning bristles. "Can I break the rules and ask you a personal question?" she said.

"Try me."

"Do all the girls come when they do it with you?"

"The reason that question is against the rules is that it doesn't have a tactful answer."

"Tell me the truth, then," she said, looking at him.

"The truth is that they all seem to, but I can't tell when they're faking it, because I don't much care."

"I bet it's usually real."

Piers got interested in the conversation. "Now why do you say that?" he asked.

"Because you're handsome, and fit, you're kind, and you're clean. And . . . you're straight."

"What do you mean—straight?"

She turned on to her back and looked at the ceiling. "You really don't know?"

"Really."

"Most of the men who use the agency don't just want to fuck, you know," she said. Piers could sense a hint of bitterness in her voice. "They always want you to beat them, or pretend to be a schoolgirl or their mother or a dog or something. That's why they have to pay for girls."

Piers sat up in bed. "Good Lord!" he said. "Do you really mean *most* of them?"

"Sure."

"I never cease to be amazed at how little of life I know," Piers said reflectively.

"I know I could lose my job for telling you this sort of thing. We're never supposed to talk to clients about other clients."

"I can see why."

"So you see, that's why you're special."

"Yes."

"And a mystery."

Piers looked startled. "Why?"

"Because you have call-girls. A man like you could have an endless string of girls for the asking. My God, I would get fired for this conversation. But Piers, why do you pay for it?"

"It's simple. I need sex from time to time, I like beautiful young women who know all about it, and my income is such that £100 is a small sum to pay for a night of pleasure. What I don't need is love. I don't want to fall in love. It's messy and emotional, and I'm not very good at it. So I take pleasure in a woman, give her £100, and keep my life nice and tidy."

She looked thoughtful for a minute, then smiled at him again. "You know, it's you who is supposed to ask what a nice person like me is doing this for. We have reversed roles."

Piers kissed her lightly, and sprang out of bed. "Good fun, though, wasn't it?" he said. He went into the bathroom.

While he shaved he listened to the girl humming in the shower. He recognised the tune as coming from the Beethoven he had played her last night.

He studied the face in the shaving mirror. It was three years since he and Palmer had met face-to-face. What differences would Palmer see in him? First he would notice the silver streaks which had started to appear in his straight, neat hair: in the sideboards and above the ears. He would see that the hair was a little longer: now it only just cleared the shirt collar. If he was observant—which he was—he would see one or two new lines in the high forehead.

Roper scraped lather off his long chin. In the unlikely event that he smiled at Palmer, he would display a newly capped tooth.

He wiped his face clean and splashed it with a very faintly scented cologne. In the bedroom, the girl was making up her face. Roper dressed in a Prince of Wales check suit, black and white, with his usual white shirt and black knitted tie. As he was pulling on his calf-length black socks, the girl said: "You should wear red socks with that suit." Piers shuddered with horror. He laced his brogues and went into the kitchen.

When the girl arrived in the kitchen, looking stunning despite the fact that she wore the clothes she had turned up in last night, Piers put a plate of scrambled eggs in front of her.

They ate in silence, then Piers poured coffee from a percolator. He sat and smoked while the girl devoured toast and marmalade.

"You don't eat much," she remarked as she spread her fifth slice with Normandy butter and coarse-cut marmalade.

"You shouldn't," he said. "At present you take enough exercise to burn it all up, but in ten years' time it will be forming ugly layers around your thighs, upper arms, and abdomen."

"You're a hypochondriac."

"No. I'm never ill. The word for people like me is valetudinarian."

"Obsessed about your health. Except that you smoke and drink, both heavily."

"That's why I need to worry about it," Piers said with a smile.

The girl wiped her fingers on a paper table napkin. "Can I ring for a cab?"

"Let me drive you home. I'm going out now."

"It's against the rules. You're not supposed to find out where I live."

"We've broken all the other rules."

"Alright. Thanks."

It was eight o'clock when Roper dropped the girl outside a house in Kensington. A few minutes later he was on the M4, heading west. The weather was cold and dry, and the road was practically deserted.

He kept the convertible Bentley at a steady 70 mph. The slow pace was a minor irritant, but if he was caught speeding by the police there would be a record of where he was on that Saturday morning: and wherever records were kept, determined people could get at them. If Roper had been fond of proverbs, his favourite would have been "Discretion is the better part of valour". He was not fond of proverbs.

The Bentley, which had cost all of a year's salary, was one of the things which nourished the myth that Piers had a large private income from his father's estate. It was a useful myth, and Piers encouraged it.

In fact his father had lived well and died poor. He had told Piers that he intended to spend all his money before he died, and that he had done. Not long after his father told him that, Roper had met Palmer for the first time.

He saw the speedometer needle had climbed to 85, and eased his foot off the accelerator. He opened a compartment beside his seat which contained a dozen or so cartridge tapes. He selected a piano concerto, and plugged it into the tapedeck. As the music from the speakers in the doors filled the car, Piers thought back to the time he had met Palmer.

After three years at Oxford and five in Army Intelligence, Roper was equipped for two professions: mathematics and spying. He joined a large food manufacturer as a marketing trainee, and spent six months selling frozen peas to grocers in the Midlands. Head Office, rather surprised he was still with the company, called him in. He told them how to increase sales by five per cent simply by altering the shape of the packets. That also surprised them, because a marketing consultancy had just told them the same thing and charged several thousand pounds for the information. They fired the consultants and promoted Roper. He then realised he was expected to spend the next few years dreaming up ways of

32

selling more frozen peas.

He had been sent to a trade conference in Birmingham which Palmer also attended. The conference was very dull, and he and Palmer had spent most of the time drinking.

Palmer looked a formidable character even then, with his large bald head, steel-rimmed spectacles and broad shoulders. He had his own company: Commercial Intelligence Services, which prepared market reports on things like the demand for soap flakes in Ghana and the availability of long-term financing for hamburger franchises.

They were attacking a bottle of whisky in Roper's hotel room when Palmer dropped his bombshell. He began by saying: "Do you know your company is bribing a middle-management executive in Hobson's, your main rivals, for confidential information?"

"Rubbish," Piers said.

"Don't you get a monthly prognosis of the opposition's plans?"

"Yes, but—"

"Your last one told you they were planning a new range of packs. Yet they haven't even printed them yet. How do you think your company found out?"

Piers was annoyed. "Leaving aside the question of how you know what's in my monthly reports, why would you know how we got the information?"

"That's my speciality—knowing things I shouldn't," Palmer replied.

"That's no answer," Piers said. He got up.

"Sit down," Palmer said in a conciliatory voice. "And listen. I came to this conference specifically to meet you. I want you to work for me. As a spy."

Roper looked at the other man, his mouth agape. He started to say something, then stopped. Instead, he filled up his glass with whisky and drank half of it straight off. "How do you know about the man in Hobson's?" he said.

"I recruited him, and I pay him," Palmer replied. "I have a contract with your company."

"And now you want to bribe me for inside information you can give to Hobson's?" said Piers incredulously.

"Certainly not. I never accept contracts from the rivals of my existing clients," said Palmer. "And I wouldn't waste you on frozen peas anyway."

"How would you use me?"

"You would have to go and work for whatever company I wanted information from. You would set up an intelligence network and send me reports. I would pay you five times whatever you drew in salary from the firm in question.

"Every top firm now indulges in industrial espionage, Piers. Mostly their operations are crude and unreliable. We are thoroughly professional."

"Why did you pick me?"

"Your training. A first in maths at Oxford, an impressive career in Army Intelligence. Your disposition. And the fact that you do not relish spending your life marketing peas—or soapsuds, or margarine, or peppermint sweets. One other thing —you want to earn a lot more than you get at present."

Once the initial shock had worn off, Piers had found the proposition enormously attractive. To have turned traitor within the firm he was already working for would have been dishonourable; but to get a job with a firm specifically for the purpose of spying on them was a completely different thing.

He had asked for time to think about it, although he knew immediately what his answer would be.

He had changed jobs every two or three years, just like any other fast-rising young executive. Palmer's organisation had gone from strength to strength, Piers had gathered, although he never learned much about it. He lived well on his very high income, and dedicated himself to his secret profession.

His memories took him all the way to Newport. He came off the end of the motorway and stopped at the first lay-by to

34

consult his map. He frowned when he saw there was no way he could avoid the centre of Cardiff. He looked at his watch: it was 11 am. He drove on.

The rain had started in East Monmouthshire, and it was now coming down steadily. Roper switched the radio on to counter the hypnotic sweep of the windscreen wipers.

An inner ring road, too new to be on the map, speeded his progress through the capital city. At its western outskirts he turned off the A48 and aimed for the coast road.

It was ten to twelve when he stopped the car near a caravan park on a cliff top. The rain was lashing in from the sea, driven by a high wind. Roper took his hat and raincoat from the back seat and struggled to put them on before getting out of the car. He locked up and looked around him.

He saw a yellow building, boarded up against the winter, with a faded sign saying "Teas—Ices—Beach Trays" swinging above the door. Beside it a path ran down between the trees. Roper followed it.

The path became quite steep, and the stone slabs which formed the steps were treacherously wet. He was forced to tread carefully, in an exaggerated tip-toe, to prevent his leather soles slipping.

When the steps ended he found himself on a rocky beach. He looked around and saw no one. He took a cigarette from his raincoat pocket, put it in his mouth, and found his lighter. He cupped his hands around the cigarette and dipped it in the high-pressure flame. Then he pushed his hat more firmly on to his head and walked down the beach to the edge of the sea.

He watched the endlessly fascinating op-art of the waves for several minutes. Then he became aware of a figure standing beside him. He turned and saw Palmer.

"Morning," Roper said.

"Filthy, isn't it," Palmer replied. He, too, was wearing a coat and hat, and he was also armed with a large umbrella, which he held partly over Roper.

35

"Sorry to bring you all this way," Palmer continued. "I was flying to Cardiff anyway this weekend, and the airport's just a mile up the road from here."

"Yes. I passed it. Don't apologise. We can be sure no casual observers will see us here." It was of paramount importance that no one should know there was any connection between them.

"Mind you, for any less-than-casual observer our meeting on a Welsh beach in the middle of winter would be a clincher. Still, I know I was not followed. And if you were being followed the game would be up already."

Roper looked at his boss. There was a barely detectable note of weariness in his voice as he rehearsed the risks. Piers wondered whether Palmer was feeling the effects of a lifetime of computing minor probabilities, taking scarcely-necessary precautions, erring on the side of prudence.

He threw the end of his cigarette in the sea and watched it bob on the surf until it disappeared. Then he said: "What's the contract for Holmes?"

"It's our American friends, Midwest Autos. You know they've just bought into the other big British-owned car manufacturers. I knew they would find an amateurish intelligence set-up, since we weren't working for the company they bought."

"Was anyone?"

"Only the ICA." Palmer was referring to another industrial espionage outfit, run by a young Irishman called Michael Lennon, which he held in deep contempt.

"Has Lennon got an operation in Holmes?"

"Yes. The Americans don't know that I know about it. We've also got a small operation going, mainly with people who resign, and shop-floor employees. At the moment we and Lennon are supplying the Americans with information of roughly the same grade. As soon as you move in, that will change. But just to make sure, I want you to smash Lennon's operation as soon as possible."

"Any particular sort of stuff the Americans want?"

"Nothing unusual. Research stuff, prototypes, styling ideas, early details of forthcoming models."

"Why have they retained Lennon as well as us?"

"They're playing a game. I told them we were better, but they wouldn't take my word for it. They're setting us up against the Irishman to see who performs better."

Roper shivered. The heavy rain had now soaked through the bottoms of his trousers and his calves felt damp. It was also running off his hat and down his neck. He took a handkerchief from his pocket and wiped his face.

Palmer continued: "Our clients didn't mention it, but there is one thing I want you to particularly look at. They have rivals in the States who must be always considering the possibility of buying British. If you get any whiff of a move like that, let me know fast."

"Sure."

"The thing is, I'm positive the ICA haven't got a man in at such a high level as us. Information like that would prove to the Americans that we are as good as we say. After all, Lennon's operatives are all roughnecks really."

Roper had his doubts about that, but he kept silent. Instead he said: "How shall I report?"

"Same way. I think it's safe."

Their method of communication relied on the traditional integrity of the English club. At a pre-arranged time, Roper would put an envelope containing his report into the "P" pidgeon-hole at the club. He would sit at the bar, where he could see the letter-rack, until Palmer came along and picked it up, which was usually about five minutes later.

"Fine. Now, what shall I do about IBC?"

"Ah, yes. Now that front has quietened down a lot lately. You've been supplying good information, but the competing companies in the field seem to be carving out their individual markets."

37

"In other words, it needs a lower-grade operation."

"Right. I've already put a sleeper in. Junior executive called Hammond."

"I've met him. So he's one of ours?"

"Yes. I want you to activate him—"

"No," Roper interrupted.

Palmer raised one of his grey eyebrows.

Roper said: "There's no point in his knowing my identity. Much safer for me to pass him the information through you. I can list you the names of the people I use. Hammond can just approach them and tell them he's taken over."

"Of course. Much better. I should have thought of that." Roper detected the note of weariness again.

"You know, it's getting more difficult for me to operate," Palmer said in a more conversational tone. "There must be fifty top businessmen who know what sort of operation I run. Anybody I'm seen speaking to must become suspect." He grinned. "Naturally, I talk to Lennon's men whenever I get a chance." He became more serious again. "Not that it seems to worry the man."

There was a silence, and Roper polluted the ocean with another cigarette end. Then Palmer said: "Do you realise what would happen if I sold Commercial Intelligence Services? I'd get a whacking price for it, because of all the lucrative consultancy contracts we have, for which we seem to do so little. Then the poor sod who bought it would find none of them renewed." He laughed.

He looked at Roper, expecting some kind of response. Piers did not know what to say, so he kept silent.

Palmer said: "Let me know what salary Holmes gives you." They had always kept to that first informal promise of five times Roper's official earnings. "I think we've covered everything." Palmer's voice became businesslike again, the brief lowering of the mask over as quickly as it had come. "Give me five minutes then come up. I shall be well away."

38

Roper nodded silently, and Palmer turned away and walked over the pebbles towards the cliff.

Roper lit a cigarette and stared out over the Bristol Channel. He went over the conversation again, mentally card-indexing the various instructions, making outline plans for carrying them out. By force of habit, he also scrutinised the things Palmer had said for subtleties, innuendoes, and hidden messages. The mysterious parts of the dialogue he filed away in his mind, against the day when more information would turn puzzle into data.

He was particularly intrigued by the weariness which had crept into Palmer's tone on two separate occasions: but it was too slight to make much sense. Still Piers speculated about it, figuring possible explanations and searching for other clues to go with it.

He tossed his cigarette into the sea, throwing it as far out as he could. He looked down at the water. As he watched, a small wave rushed at his feet and deposited two burnt-out fag-ends in front of his toes. He turned around and followed Palmer's footsteps across the sand to where they met the rocks.

# Three

Roper steered the Bentley off the A12 and glanced at the dashboard clock. Laurence Dean had suggested he arrive at about 11.30 am, so Piers intended to get to Dean's country house at exactly 11.30. He had twenty minutes to cover the five or six miles left.

He reached across to the passenger seat and picked up the memorandum on which his secretary had written Dean's message. The directions read: "Turn left just before the river. The house is two miles along that road, on the right-hand side." The vagueness of the instructions was an indication, Piers assumed, that the house was hard to miss.

He found the left turn without trouble. There was a row of oldish council houses on the left, and then the village petered out, and the road became a twisting country lane. Piers memorised his odometer reading and looked out for a large house.

When he had gone another five miles he decided he must have missed it. The clock said 11.25. He stopped the car and recollected the route he had followed.

First he had passed one or two cottages, too small for a weekend house party. There had been a larger house which might fit the bill, but the nameplate outside gave the name of a doctor and details of surgery hours. Next had come a muddy track leading to what was plainly a farmhouse, with barns and tractors. After that, nothing.

Clearly the house was concealed from the main road. In the flat Essex countryside very little was hidden from the road: therefore he only had to work out where a house might be concealed.

He recalled a clump of trees in between the doctor's house and the farm. He closed his eyes and pictured it. There was a break in the trees which might have been a driveway. He turned the car around and drove back, taking the tight bends rather fast.

It was 11.29 when he stopped the car outside the house.

It was a Georgian farmhouse which had apparently been owned by a series of wealthy farmers who had each rebuilt parts, modernised, and added bits.

A donkey was grazing on the lawn in front of the house, and a man in overalls up a ladder was renewing the cream-coloured paint of one wing. In the forecourt Piers saw parked a Rolls, a Mercedes, and one of Holmes' three-litre executive Diplomats.

Roper got out of the car, leaving his keys in the ignition. Dean appeared from around the side of the house and walked across, his arm extended for a handshake.

"Roper! I thought I heard a car. Welcome. Find the place alright?"

Piers shook his hand. "Yes, although a map would have saved a little time."

"Didn't you get one? I asked my secretary to send you one. Everyone who comes here gets one—place is such a swine to find. Never mind, you made it. Come in."

He escorted Piers to the front door. A butler came out as they went in, and Dean said: "Bring Mr. Roper's case, please, Haskell."

Piers added: "The boot is unlocked."

"Very good, sir," the man replied.

Dean stopped on the polished wood floor of the hall. The stairs were directly opposite the door, and there were two more doors on the left and right of the small, square hall. Piers noticed a third door beside the staircase.

"Come into the drawing-room when you've changed," Dean

41

said, pointing at the door on the right. He glanced at Roper's plain grey suit. "We're quite casual here at the weekend," he said. He was wearing a brown tweed jacket and fawn trousers.

The butler came in with Roper's case. Dean said: "Haskell will show you your room." Piers followed the butler up the stairs. The man led him along a carpeted corridor which ran above the drawing-room.

They turned a corner. "This is your bathroom, sir," said Haskell. "I hope you won't mind sharing, as the house is full."

"Not at all," Piers replied. He followed the butler into a bedroom. "Who am I sharing it with?"

"Miss Shipley, sir," the butler replied. Roper raised his eyebrows. "Miss Estelle Shipley," he amplified. "She's here with her father, Lord Shipley."

Roper nodded. Lord Shipley was the Chairman of Holmes. So he was interested enough in Roper to spend a weekend roughing it in the country with his Managing Director. Piers wondered just what was the significance of this appointment to the company. He postponed the problem until he had more data.

Haskell said: "Would you like me to unpack while you have a wash, sir?"

"Thank you," Piers said. He put a towel over his arm and went along the corridor to the bathroom.

When he came back the butler had gone. Piers took off his shirt and replaced it with an identical white one. He changed into a grey herringbone jacket and black trousers, and put on one of the three black knitted ties he had brought with him. Then he combed his hair, loaded his cigarette case, and went downstairs.

The only person in the drawing-room was a girl of about 25. She had chin-length blonde hair, and wore a check shirt and flared trousers. "You must be Miss Shipley," said Roper.

"Estelle," the girl said. "And you're Piers Roper. Drink?"

"Scotch, please." Piers wondered why Dean was not in the room to introduce him. The girl handed him a glass and he poured water in it. "I see we're sharing a bathroom," he said by way of small talk.

"That's the least of the trials you're in for," she replied with a smile. "I'm just here to disguise the appointments board as a house party."

Piers sipped his drink and said nothing.

"So you're the chap this whole thing is in aid of," the girl continued.

Roper decided he had to say something. "That's one of those things everyone knows and no one says," he offered.

She bowed mockingly. "Reprimand acknowledged," she said.

Dean walked in, to Roper's relief. "Sorry, Roper," he said. "I see Estelle has been looking after you."

The girl said: "Let me look after you, Larry. What will it be?"

"Ah, good girl. Gin and tonic, please."

Piers studied the girl as she made the drink. Her clothes were good, but she was far too made-up for a Saturday in the country. She had spent some time on her eyes, with shadow, mascara, and some kind of highlighter; and she wore lipstick and foundation as well as face powder. Then Piers realised why: her face was quite plain, and it was only the make-up which rescued her from ugliness.

Two more men and a woman came in. Roper recognised the tall, grey-haired man with thick spectacles as Lord Shipley, and the elegant woman at his side was Lady Mary Hollowood, wife of the third person, Sir Trevor Hollowood, Financial Director of Holmes.

As he shook hands all around Piers matched the people with the cars he had seen in the drive. The Rolls would be Shipley's, the Mercedes would belong to Dean, and the Holmes Diplomat would be driven by Hollowood.

Piers decided to call Hollowood Sir Trevor, his wife Lady Mary, and Lord Shipley just plain "sir". That meant he could not call Dean sir. Dean called him Roper, he recalled. Very well: he would call him Dean.

Estelle served them all drinks, and Piers chatted to Lady Mary. At one o'clock the butler announced lunch.

As they crossed the hall to the dining-room, Dean said to Roper in a low voice: "Hope you don't mind sharing a bathroom, Roper. This place is too small, you know. We should have moved out ages ago, but Charlotte likes it. She'll be in here." They entered the room. "Let me introduce you. Charlotte, my dear, meet Piers Roper." Piers shook hands with a tired-looking woman who was as short and almost as stout as her husband.

When Piers sat down he immediately noticed that he did not have a soup-spoon. In its place was an ordinary silver dessert-spoon. He immediately dismissed the possibility that Dean was short of dining silver: if that were the case, surely either Dean himself or his wife would have been given the odd spoon.

He could do one of two things: decline the soup, and cover the error; or ask for a soup spoon. When Haskell came around with the tureen of soup Piers said quietly: "A soup spoon, please, Haskell."

The butler looked startled. "I'm terribly sorry, sir," he said. He picked up the dessert-spoon, went to the cabinet at the side of the room, and returned with a soup-spoon.

The rest of the company appeared not to have noticed the quiet exchange, except for Estelle, who gave Piers a wink.

While they were drinking the soup, Dean said to the butler: "Serve the burgundy, if you would, Haskell."

Piers frowned. The soup was lobster: no one would want to drink Burgundy with it. He ignored his wine until the meat was served.

He continued to make small talk with Lady Mary, who was on his left, while he inwardly reviewed his progress so far. A

44

series of trivial events made a pattern, and Estelle had given him the clue which made sense of the pattern. She had said that sharing a bathroom was the least of the trials he was in for: and the word "trial" had a double meaning, Roper now realised.

The business of the soup-spoon, and Dean's gaffe with the wine, were both tests of Piers' social behaviour. If he had drunk soup with a dessert-spoon, or tasted his wine before the meat was served, he would have revealed himself to be socially clumsy.

Finding the house had probably also been a test, he decided. It was all rather infantile, but then Managing Directors were permitted their eccentricities.

He wondered what would be the next hazard on the obstacle course.

After lunch Roper strolled in the grounds with Lord Shipley. Piers was wary of the Tory peer. His hearty manner was affected by a lot of aristocracy: in some cases to conceal a dullness bordering on stupidity, and in others to disguise a keen, Machiavellian brain.

"How did you get into marketing?" he asked Roper.

"Frozen peas," Piers replied.

"Ah."

"When I came out of the army I did a stint selling for Easipax. I made one or two bright suggestions and they promoted me to Head Office." Roper knew he was expected to boast a little, but a lot would depend on how gracefully he did it. He struck a note of diffidence, and pretended a casual interest in the fine avenue of trees down which they walked.

Shipley nodded his grey head. "Interesting how we make some of the most important decisions of our lives quite by accident."

Piers did not think that remark required a reply. They came to the end of the avenue. It should have led somewhere: it was too grand to stand on its own, like a staircase in a

45

bungalow. But at its end was a landscaped lawn criss-crossed by paths.

Piers studied the layout for a moment. "No doubt the road used to cut across here."

"I believe so," Shipley replied. "When it was just a track. Then the council took it over and shifted it, leaving the house with a grand drive leading nowhere." He started along one of the paths, and Roper followed his lead.

"And how do you find life at IBC?"

The question was designed to reveal his reasons for wanting to leave, Piers realised. It was important not to run his employer down.

"It's been a very exciting time," he said.

"Has been?"

"Yes. There was a time, you know, when the marketing war in the computer field was almost as hot as soap powder. A little more dignified, of course—more of the rapier than the cutlass, as it were—but equally fierce."

"And now?"

Piers thought it wise to let Shipley pump him, rather than volunteer information. He did not want to seem too eager to talk about his business.

"Like most wars, it ended with the drawing of boundaries and an uneasy peace. You see, the opposition had a lot of muscle. Their parent organisation, in the USA, were—and still are—leaders in the field. We could not hope to rival them in technical advance. When I went to IBC I thought we should let them have the big stuff.

"We concentrated on fairly unsophisticated machines that we could sell a lot of: computers for payroll work, desk-top calculators, and so on. And we ran a line of software to match. We left areas like scientific work, real-time operations, leasing, to the Americans.

"It worked well, as a marketing strategy. But life became a little less exciting." Roper had spoken carefully, choosing his

46

words, subtly taking credit for himself—he had used the first person pronoun only once, intentionally—and saying in a roundabout manner that he was looking for a new challenge.

"You didn't consider fighting fire with fire—getting some American help to compete with the Americans?"

The question caught Piers off-guard. It was not a logical one. Its link with what had gone before was too slight, and its answer was common knowledge. Piers said: "Politics precluded that." But he continued to puzzle over the motive behind the question. He felt it might have something to do with what Palmer had told him—Palmer had used that phrase, "the Americans", quite a lot. Piers had a feeling that what came next would be important.

"The motor industry has parallel problems," Shipley said. Piers waited for him to enlarge on that, but the two of them walked on in silence.

Shipley stopped in front of a tall, graceful tree which was decorated with a parasitic creeper of some kind which twined around its trunk. "Funny things, creepers," he said inconsequentially.

"A bit like the Americans," Piers said in the same conversational tone.

Shipley turned and looked sharply at him. "How?"

Piers smiled, concealing his awareness of the importance of what he would say. "When you're strong, they're very attractive and present no threat. But during a drought they can be fatal. You may be left with a flourishing creeper and a dead tree."

Shipley nodded. "Rather well put," he said pleasantly. He added: "Although a very dubious piece of horticulture." He smiled and walked on.

Roper had the feeling he had crossed an important bridge.

Sir Trevor Hollowood picked up his king from the chess-board. "I'm afraid I'm not giving you much of a game, Piers," he said. "I think I should retire gracefully."

Roper smiled pleasantly. He had beaten Sir Trevor easily, three times running. He began to rearrange the pieces on the onyx chess-table.

"Would you two like some tea?" inquired Lady Mary from the other side of the room. Haskell had brought in a tray a few minutes before.

"Not for me, dear," Sir Trevor said. "I must glance at the newspaper," he added, and picked up The Telegraph. He ensconced himself in a corner chair and settled down to read.

"I will have some, if I may," Piers said. Lady Mary got up to pour. "No, let me," Piers intervened. He crossed to the table and poured tea from the ornate china pot. "Would you like some more?" he asked her. She accepted, and he poured for her.

"Thank you," she said. "You'd make a capable housewife, Mr. Roper. I suppose it comes of being a confirmed bachelor."

"It comes of being a bachelor. I'm not so confirmed," he replied.

"Ah! Eligible, then."

"Oh dear. The phrase conjured up a picture of a rather self-centred young man preening himself at a debutante's ball."

"How would you describe yourself, then?"

Piers knew he had to give a plausible answer to the question. This conversation was just another in the series of tests. Lady Mary wanted to make sure he was neither a homosexual nor a Casanova.

"I think I'd be forced to used another cliché. I'm waiting for the right woman."

"It's been a long wait."

"Better than a bad choice. I wonder if you realise how fortunate you and Sir Trevor are, Lady Mary. The people who pick the right partner early in life are in a minority."

"Do you disapprove of marriage?"

48

"On the contrary. I just think it should be taken rather seriously."

She changed tack. "I suppose you have some substitute—you're obsessed with toy soldiers, or Norman architecture, or fishing."

"I don't think so."

"But you must have some burning enthusiasm—all bachelors do. Foreign stamps? Golf? Deep-sea diving?"

"I like chess, crosswords, Mahler, Impressionist painting. But I would call none of them enthusiasms. I work quite hard, you know." He added a smile to counter the smugness of his last remark.

"Ah. Dedicated to your profession."

"Not dedicated. Dedication means one would do it for nothing. I do it for a great deal of money. And because I like it."

She changed tack again. "I was admiring your car," she said. "So much more exciting than a plain Rolls."

She had noticed that his car indicated an income much higher than he could afford on what IBC paid him. And it seemed her brief was wider than just his sex life. Lady Mary had been briefed to cover his personal life, Piers decided.

He said nothing, preferring to let her make the running. He set down his cup and offered her a cigarette from his case. "I'm afraid I don't have any filter tips," he apologised.

"That's all right." She took one of her own cigarettes from her handbag, and he lit it for her. His expensive silver lighter did not escape her notice.

"A Bentley is a bit big for town, though, isn't it?"

"I do some travelling. In fact I rarely use the car in town. I've a house in Scotland, and I go there quite often."

"A house in Scotland and a Bentley? IBC must pay you well."

The interrogation had become overt, and Piers decided he should react to it. He gave an embarrassed grin, and said: "They do, but not that well. Fortunately I don't rely on my salary."

"Dear me," she said. "You must think me rather inquisi-
tive."

Sir Trevor emerged from behind the newspaper. "Piers may
not, but I do," he said. "It's just as well the poor chap doesn't
know any state secrets, or you'd have had them out of him by
now. Time we went up to change."

Piers looked at his watch.

Sir Trevor said: "Dinner's usually quite early here, Piers.
Lounge suits, too."

"Thank you."

Sir Trevor nodded and escorted his wife up the stairs. Piers
lit a cigarette and stretched out his legs. It was dark outside,
and the room was lit by a number of table-lamps scattered
around. Piers looked at the cocktail cabinet, and decided he
ought not to help himself.

Haskell came in. "I'll make up the fire, sir, if I may," he
said.

"Go ahead, Haskell," said Piers.

The butler paused in front of the grate. He turned to Roper
and said: "Would you like a drink, sir?"

"Haskell, you're a mind-reader. Scotch with a little water."

The butler poured the drink, handed it to Piers, and pro-
ceeded to work on the fire. "I sometimes think you have to be
a mind-reader, to be a good butler," he offered.

"I'm sure," said Piers. It was interesting that Dean's ser-
vants should be so ready to show signs of dissatisfaction. Piers
suspected that Mrs. Dean did not manage them very well.

Haskell went out. Piers sipped the whisky and reviewed his
performance so far. He had passed the initiative test, the
etiquette test, and satisfied Lady Mary of the unimpeachability
of his personal life. She probably knew she had not quite got
the measure of him—that question about his having some
enthusiasm apart from his job had been rather close to the
mark.

And after the chess match Sir Trevor probably thought him a good brain. The only thing that remained to trouble Piers was his conversation with Lord Shipley in the grounds.

Once again, he had the feeling that he had passed some sort of test out there: but he could not work out just what he had done right.

He dropped his cigarette in the ashtray, swallowed the rest of the whisky, and went upstairs to change.


Roper handed Mrs. Dean a drink. She was dressed well, though without any flair, and her hair and make-up were competent. The money and position which were hers would have given most women self-confidence: but she always looked a little uneasy.

Piers said: "You have a very good cook, Mrs. Dean. Dinner was marvellous. In fact I'm enjoying myself very much."

She smiled gracefully. "Thank you," she said.

Piers turned back to Estelle, who handed him a glass. She said in a low voice: "You have a nice touch." Piers decided the girl was altogether too candid.

Piers walked over to where the men were sitting, in a semi-circle around the fireplace. He sat in an easy chair which had plainly been left empty for him. Dean pushed a box of cigars his way, but he shook his head and took out his cigarette case.

Lord Shipley was saying: "There are two sorts of long-term planning: the one facile and the other misleading. You can pick trends at random and extrapolate them—say petrol is getting dearer so cars will get smaller, or people are getting wealthier therefore cars will get bigger. That method is useless because it is too easy.

"The alternative is to collect a lot of facts and figures by market research: study trends in demand, all that sort of thing. Then you have to project your curves so far that they become pure conjecture; yet you believe them because of the mass of statistics which goes into them. That method is useless because it is too difficult."

He paused, and puffed his cigar into life. "Anyway, I've never known any piece of long-term planning which didn't have to be scrapped long before anyone acted on it."

"It's not that bad," said Dean. "You're exaggerating. There has to be some kind of serious forward thinking in an industry as weighty as ours."

"So long as nobody really believes in it," Shipley insisted. "If you look at any of the major advances in automotive production since the war, you'll find nobody foresaw any of them. Take the Mini—a piece of imaginative genius that left us all with egg on our faces." Roper was startled to see envy flicker momentarily on Shipley's face. Then his expression became semi-jocular again. "Take the safety scare—if long-term planning does anything, it should warn of things like that. Expensive things."

Sir Trevor put in: "One thing we can foresee at present: so much new research is being done—basic, let's-take-a-whole-new-look-at-it stuff—that the present form of the motor car is doomed. There has to be a revolution. Otherwise we're all wasting an awful lot of money."

"Can't agree," said Dean brusquely. "We produce a high-efficiency, low-cost form of transport that is safer than anything that has gone before—horse-drawn carriages caused far more accidents than cars—and has given ordinary people undreamed-of mobility. It's taken a combination of genius, in the pioneers, and the might of capitalism, to get us here. A few scientists with their heads in the clouds won't reproduce that phenomenon in a few years. The petrol car is here to stay for a long time."

Sir Trevor said: "What do you think, Piers?"

Roper crossed his legs. "I think we can predict a lot of things," he began. "The energy crisis, the safety boom, lower speed limits—they're all more or less permanent features of the scene. But economics is likely to overshadow them all.

"Since we're being speculative, consider this: Western capitalism is now at full stretch. Economic growth as a political priority is on its last legs. America and Britain have just about abandoned it, Japan pursues it at enormous social cost, Europe struggles on with grave doubts.

"Then there's population. Large factors like this mean a lot more than styling trends and consumer preferences. The population of Britain has levelled out, and it's about to start falling. We know what that means: a higher average age, more pensioners to support, a permanent slackening of demand.

"So it's a possibility, at the least, that we should be preparing for a slow downhill glide into the twenty-first century. We will no longer be able to rely upon a continual increase in production volume. Built-in obsolescence will become obsolete. New models every half-year will become a thing of the past. To keep overheads down, we'll have to produce a more standard car, sell it over a longer period of time, and make it less sophisticated, not more. The only way of increasing profits will be to increase profit margins—and in a slump that means cutting costs, since you can't put prices up."

Lord Shipley looked thoughtful. "That *is* an interesting conjecture," he said.

Dean stood up. He looked around at the men. "I see we're all drinking brandy," he said. "I'll bring the bottle over here and we can help ourselves."

Sir Trevor continued the discussion. "For any government to abandon the policy of economic growth would be political suicide."

Piers saw that the remark was directed at him. He was walking a tightrope now. It had been necessary to say something fairly startling—they expected him to make an impression. But it would be easy to sound slightly fanatical. He needed to be a bit self-deprecating now.

"There's a good chance that we will continue to make do and mend, economically. We've done that for a good few

53

years now. But suppose we can't. Economic realities have a way of imposing themselves on politics.

"This much can't be denied: economic growth is synonymous with the fastest possible depletion of natural resources. And natural resources are limited, at least from a practical point of view."

"Therefore economic growth is limited," Sir Trevor finished.

Lord Shipley leaned forward in his chair, his cigar forgotten. "Why did you say 'from a practical point of view'?"

"Because what is limited is not, strictly speaking, energy. It's coal, oil, sunlight, raw materials. Available energy, to be accurate. But in theory there's enough energy locked in the atom to keep us going for several million years. Perhaps we'll find new fuel techniques before the slump comes."

Shipley nodded. Suddenly Piers saw Estelle, leaning against the back of her father's chair. He realised she had been listening to the conversation for a long time.

She said: "You puzzle me, Piers. How do you reconcile all that with the way you earn your living? After all, marketing is the art of making people buy more—that's to say, making them consume more energy."

"Quite right," Piers replied. "But I shall be in my sixties before the slump comes, if it ever does. By the time it really starts to bite, I'll be dead."

He paused, quite serious now. "And I have no children," he finished quietly.

The men spent Sunday morning on the golf course. Dean played badly and lost cheerfully, as if he were used to it. Roper and Sir Trevor played only passably; Lord Shipley won.

"D'you play much, Roper?" Dean asked him as they strolled back to the clubhouse.

"No," Piers replied. "I found out years ago that I was never going to be very good."

"So did I, but I'm addicted to the damn game," Dean

replied. "Does you good, you know, to have a hobby you're appallingly bad at. Most relaxing. Psychologically stabilising."

"Really?" It was an interesting thought, but Piers was pre-occupied. He was reviewing his performance the previous evening. His iron self-control had lapsed momentarily, and he had found himself thinking seriously about the discussion, instead of about how he was presenting himself.

The effect had been mixed, he concluded. Shipley had loved it: that kind of intellectual discussion fascinated him. Sir Trevor, too, had seemed to think that what Piers had said was perceptive and interesting.

But Dean had not. The Managing Director maintained an I'm-a-plain-man self-image: he liked to think he had no truck with airy-fairy philosophising. It was partly bluff, to make people over-confident; and partly defensive, for he really did feel uneasy with academic phraseology. So Piers had lost points with him. He would have to win them back.

Shipley bought a round of drinks in the bar, and they discussed the game for a while. Sir Trevor said: "Only good thing to be said for it, it's healthy exercise."

"Ah, you haven't been bitten by the bug," Shipley said. "Mind you, if it were not for golf I would get no exercise at all."

"You seem very fit, Piers," Sir Trevor said. "What do you do for exercise?"

"Golf is too time-consuming for me, normally," Roper replied. "I do some exercises with weights."

"Bad for the heart," Dean put in. "Still, not at your age, I don't suppose."

As the healthiest among them—and quite patently so—Piers was on shaky ground: it would be very easy to say something offensive. He looked at his watch. "Well, we have an hour or so at the bar now, in which to wipe out any good which has been done by our morning's exercise," he smiled.

Dean looked at his watch. "Damn!" he exclaimed. "I clean

forgot—I promised to be at home at 12 noon to take a phone call from Melbourne. Piers—would you drive me?"

"Certainly." As they left the clubhouse, Piers had the feeling which had come to him repeatedly all weekend, that something had happened which was not quite logical. The natural thing would have been for Dean to ask his subordinate, Sir Trevor, to drive him—not his principal guest. Roper could always tell when people were manoeuvring, and Dean was doing it now.

As he got into the car, he made a quick calculation. The house was about 10 miles from the golf course, and the time was now seven minutes to twelve. He would have to drive very fast to get Dean there on time.

He turned on the engine and fastened his safety belt while Dean impatiently drummed his fingers on the leather seat. He pulled away quite fast down the drive and out into the road.

"Don't hang about," Dean said to him. "If I miss this call it may be difficult to get in touch again. You know what it's like, telephoning Australia. Bloody call has to be switched through Afghanistan, or something."

It all seemed a bit spurious, Piers thought. Perhaps this was another of Dean's tests. At first he dismissed the thought, then he forced himself to reconsider it, quickly. The only safe plan was to treat it as a test. He put his foot down.

He sped along the narrow road, making full use of the Bentley's roadholding on the corners, forcing Dean to grip the leather grab handle which dangled from the roof. He screeched around a roundabout and into an approach road for the A12. He found himself on the left-hand side of a line of cars which were bogging the inside lane. He accelerated hard and pulled in front of them. The leading car honked indignantly.

The speedometer needle passed the 100 mark. "I hope you've a good relationship with the local constabulary," Piers said to Dean.

Their turn-off approached quickly. In front of the Bentley

56

was a heavy lorry on the inside lane and a fast-moving saloon in the middle lane, engaged in overtaking the lorry. There was not quite enough space in front of the saloon for Roper to overtake it before his turn-off.

He stole a glance at Dean, and saw the Managing Director looking impatiently at his watch. Piers made a quick decision. He changed down out of overdrive and flashed his headlights. The car leapt forward with an ounce more acceleration. He flashed his left-turning trafficator. He could see the bewildered expression of the saloon's driver as he whipped past. He heaved the steering wheel over to the left and the big car swung towards the turn-off, tyres protesting shrilly. He fought to prevent a skid. The saloon car tooted in a panicky fashion. Piers thought he was not going to make it. Then he was off the main road. He swung the wheel again to straighten the car on the uphill exit road. He did not dare to touch the brakes. The rear wheels came perilously close to slipping. The slight uphill slope slowed the car by a margin, enough to avert disaster. The car settled, and Piers put his foot down again.

He glanced at Dean again, and suppressed a smile when he saw the shine of perspiration on the man's forehead. You asked for it, he thought.

He squealed around the corner in the centre of the village, noticing the stares of the locals outside the pub beside the bridge. He would have liked to look at the time, but he could not spare his attention from the task of driving.

He turned into the entrance of Dean's house and went up the twisting gravel drive between the trees with one hand on the horn. He turned past a bush into the forecourt and saw the donkey right in front of him. He swung the wheel hard and went into a broadside skid. The car stopped a foot short of the dumb animal, which walked slowly away.

Piers looked at his watch. It was a minute to twelve.

But Dean seemed to have forgotten the phone call. He sat in the passenger seat and looked at Roper. "Just how I would

57

have done it," he murmured. Piers was not sure whether he meant the whole drive or its dramatic finish.

In a louder voice Dean said: "I'm looking for a new Senior Marketing Executive. Name your price."

# Four

Roper hated Midlands towns. The modern buildings were as drab and monolithic as London's; and the older architecture looked simply squalid, lacking the aura of tradition which gave London's elderly houses and offices a saving dignity. The greed and exploitation of the industrial revolution had left London with a string of monuments to civilisation; but it had given the Midlands monuments to greed and exploitation.

On reflection, it was simply a matter of prejudice. London was home, the rest of the country a strange land. If he were honest with himself, perhaps it was not the architecture which depressed him, as much as the simple unfamiliarity of the place. But this was where cars were made, and cars were now Roper's business.

It was Friday, and his first free lunchtime in a week at the Holmes Motor Corporation. It had been a week of introductions, familiarisation, tours of departments, handshaking, the constant struggle to fit new names to new faces, and to absorb information as fast as it was doled out to him. All his lunches—and dinners, too—had been working ones, talking to busy men who could not spare any other time to meet a newcomer. Especially at a time like this.

For Roper had arrived at Holmes in the middle of a crisis. He was not yet sure of his own role in the struggle. But it had immediately become clear to him that the company was in trouble. The outstanding problem was that the sales of the Capricorn—the new car Piers had seen previewed three or four months ago in London—had been disappointingly sluggish. There was more to it than that, he was sure: but he did not know what the other elements of the crisis were.

He had pondered the problem over his lunch—an overdone steak which came from an undernourished Argentinian cow— in a restaurant in the town centre. Now he strolled around the shops, looking gloomily in the windows of estate agents' offices.

He had taken an hotel room, and planned to return to London most weekends. But he would have to find a decent house or flat somewhere fairly near the mammoth Holmes works. Hotel living, even in the town's most expensive concrete monstrosity, was uncivilised.

He could afford to run a third home now, without making demands on his capital. Holmes paid him £20,000 a year, which meant he got the phenomenal sum of £100,000 a year from Palmer's "trust fund". He would have to come up with the goods to justify that kind of money.

He reckoned he was worth it. The motor industry was a multi-million pound business, and the kind of information he could provide Holmes' rivals with would probably save them millions.

He went into a second-rate department store, more to escape the chill for a few minutes than for any other purpose. He found himself at the menswear counter, and bought a dozen pairs of plain calf-length black socks.

He could hardly believe it when he discovered he was being followed.

He made the standard checks routinely, out of habit. They came to him as naturally as looking both ways when he crossed the road. The young man in a donkey jacket had been behind him on three occasions in his aimless stroll through the shopping centre. Roper had deliberately walked past the department store, then doubled back and gone inside. Now the man was giving his concentrated attention to a display of china which, Piers was sure, he would never want to buy.

Piers walked on. If he was being followed, he was suspected. But by whom? And of what? And what had he done that was suspicious?

There was nothing. He was sure of that. He had not made a single underhand move at Holmes: it was too early. The likelihood was that he was being followed as a matter of routine.

But surely the Holmes Motor Corporation did not put a tail on every new senior executive they employed? If not, that left the ICA.

If they were on the ball, Michael Lennon's firm might well be interested in a new executive. They knew about Palmer's outfit, and presumably they knew that the Americans had hired Palmer.

Roper stole another glance at the man, and suddenly recognised his face. He had seen the fellow on one of his works tours: he strained his memory, and placed the face in the paint shop. Good.

It would be foolish to give the man the slip—for that would reveal that Roper *was* a spy. Only spies throw off tails.

No, there was a way to use the man. Piers devised a plan.

He walked along until he saw a taxi rank on the far side of the road. Checking that the donkey jacket was still in attendance, he crossed the road. He ran in front of a slow-moving bus, so that when he reached the opposite pavement the big vehicle hid him momentarily from the follower's sight. He went up to the door of the taxi and bent his head to speak to the driver.

"Would you take me to Stanton Works—Holmes'?" he said. As he spoke he watched through the windows of the cab. The donkey jacket ran across the road, plainly concerned that he had lost Roper.

"Alright, jump in," said the cabbie impatiently. Piers waited until the tail came running around the back of the cab. Then he opened the door. The man dodged to pass the door, and Piers stuck out his foot. The man went flying.

Piers helped him up. "My dear fellow, I'm terribly sorry,"

he said. Confusion and a trace of fear appeared on the man's face. Piers kept a firm grip on his arm, noticing the tell-tale spray marks of metallic bronze paint on the hand. "I simply didn't see you," he continued apologetically. "Are you all right?"

"Yes thanks," the man said breathlessly. He was in his early twenties, Piers saw. The man made an effort to disengage his arm.

Piers frowned. "You work at Holmes, don't you," he said. "Look, you must be shaken up. Let me give you a lift back." And he firmly pushed the man into the car.

The impatient driver pulled away immediately. The young man rubbed his knee.

"Bruised, I expect," Piers said. "I'm Piers Roper, the new marketing executive. This is not the ideal way to meet the staff, I don't suppose. What's your name?"

"John Coley," the man replied. He was beginning to feel extremely foolish.

"How do you do, John. Paint shop, isn't it?"

There was real fear in the man's eyes now. Piers guessed he was thinking about what would happen if his masters saw him in a taxi with the man he was supposed to be following. He suppressed a malicious grin. Coley nodded: "Paint shop."

Roper chatted on cheerfully. "What do you think of the colour range on the Capricorn?"

"Very nice."

"Pretty good, isn't it. Do you drive a Holmes?"

"I've got a Capricorn."

"Super. They must pay well in the paint shop. Ah, here we are. I'll drop you and get the cabbie to take me on to the office block." Coley got out. "Sorry about the fall," Roper called after him.

John Coley, paint shop, he said under his breath, to fix the man's name in his memory. He was quite pleased. If the company wanted to spy on its executives, they would hardly use one of their own shop-floor workers. Therefore Coley worked for Lennon. The man would probably lie about the incident to his masters, whoever they were. Even if he told them the truth, they would still only have a suspicion that Piers was working for Palmer.

But Piers himself had made a very significant discovery. He had penetrated Lennon's organisation.

He got out of the cab in front of the office block. Somehow the place still looked like a factory, as if the local architecture were infectious. He went in, nodding to the commissionaire, and took the lift to his own office.

He took off his hat and coat and said to his secretary: "Would you get me Mr. Giddins in Personnel?"

"Right away, Mr. Roper." Piers winced at the girl's thick accent, then reprimanded himself. Prejudice again.

He sat at his desk and looked at his watch. With luck, Giddins would still be at lunch.

The intercom hummed. "Mr. Giddins is not in, sir," the secretary said.

"Thank you." He went out of his office and said to the secretary: "Where is Personnel?"

"Second floor, directly underneath us."

Piers went down in the lift again. As he walked along the nylon-carpeted corridor, he passed a hot drink machine. Miniature flies buzzed around a plastic bucket which held used paper cups, and the green carpet around the machine was stained with spills of tea and instant coffee. My God, will I ever get used to it? he thought.

He walked into a general office. A door on the left said: "Personnel Officer: Miss Anne Mainwaring." A typist sat at a desk near the door. Roper said: "Is Miss Mainwaring in?"

"Yes," the girl replied.

Piers knocked on the door and walked in. The girl behind the desk inside looked up, surprised. Then she recognised him. They had met a couple of times during the week.

63

Roper said: "Mr. Giddins still at lunch?"

"He went out quite late," the girl said defensively. But I wonder just how far your loyalty to your boss extends, Piers thought. He was secretly pleased Giddins was out. He would have to answer fewer questions, dealing with a subordinate.

"Never mind, I expect you can help me. I'd like to look at an employee's file. John Coley, paint shop."

"Certainly," the girl said. She went to the door and spoke to the typist outside. Piers studied her as she returned to her desk. She had a small, very pretty head, with a turned-up nose. Her green eyes were her best feature, and her make-up emphasised them. Her hair was cut dramatically short—shorter than most men's, these days. Her frame was quite wide at the shoulders and hips. She would be fat when she was older. Then he looked harder and revised his estimate of her age: she must be thirty, he decided.

She returned his stare fearlessly. Piers made up his mind that he would use her.

Lorries roared past underneath the window. Roper got up and shut it. "You won't mind if I close the window for a moment," he said.

"Go ahead," she said, although he had already done it. "I keep it open to remind me that I'm working for a car manufacturer."

"A very good reason for keeping it shut, I should have thought," Piers said. The typist came in with a file. She passed Roper, intending to hand it to Miss Mainwaring. Piers reached out and took it.

As the typist left Miss Mainwaring said: "Thank you, Jean." Piers said nothing and opened the file.

"May I ask why you want to see that file?" the woman said.

Piers frowned. It was a presumptuous question. He said: "I must admit I'm unfamiliar with procedure here, but I think I'm entitled to look at employee's personal files."

"And I'm entitled to ask why."

"But I don't have to tell you."

"As you wish." She stood up and walked around her desk. Piers stood up and held out an arm to stop her walking away. He smiled apologetically. "I'm being a bit brusque," he said.

"I'll say you are."

"Forgive me. I'll tell you why I want to see the file."

She looked up at him coolly, then melted. "All right, Mr. Roper," she said. She returned to her chair.

"I caused this fellow a minor accident a while ago, after lunch," he said. "I opened a car door and he ran into it. I'm just wondering whether he's the litigious kind."

She tipped her head back and laughed. It was a rich, deep, almost masculine chuckle from the back of her throat; an unlikely sound from a woman with such a pretty, elfin face.

"However," Piers continued, "he's not a shop steward or a vacationing law student, so I think I'm safe." Roper had found what he was really looking for. A note in the file, made at the time the man had been taken on, said: "Recc. D. R. Briggs, foundry." Piers memorised the name and closed the file.

The woman was friendly now. "I don't suppose you've found anywhere to live yet?" she asked politely.

"No. I suspect it will be a long search. Do you know of anywhere?"

She shook her head. "'Fraid not. I spend a lot of my time in town."

"I noticed you're not afflicted with the local accent. Is London your home?"

"As much as anywhere. I go up most weekends."

"Well! You must let me give you a lift. Are you going up tonight?"

"I was planning to catch the 5.30."

"Then I will drive you, if I may."

65

She smiled again. It was a wide smile, crinkling the corners of her eyes, a smile with a sense of fun in it. "Thank you," she said.

Piers put the file on her desk and stood up. As he went to the door he said: "I appreciate your help, Miss Mainwaring."

"It's pronounced Mane-wearing, not Mannering," she said. "See you later."

When he got back upstairs, Piers stood in his own office, considering what was to be done with it. It had potential: it was big, light, and airy. The uniform green nylon carpet would have to stay, as would the mass produced Scandinavian timber desk. He would have to get rid of the black vinyl swivel chair before it broke his back: perhaps he had something at home that would do instead. The cream painted walls were acceptable. He would hang some pictures—nothing very valuable. Some modern abstracts, he decided. The row of green metal filing cabinets would have to go: he would have a word with the establishments officer.

He looked at his watch. It was time to go to Dean's office. As he left his secretary said: "Time for your meeting with Mr. Dean, sir."

He stopped and looked at her. "I'm on my way," he said. "You're late reminding me. I should tell you that I'm not in the habit of giving people second chances. If ever I'm late for an important appointment because you've failed to remind me, I shall fire you." He smiled to soften the rebuke. "Your eyelash is coming unglued," he added.

Her only redeeming quality was ugliness, he thought as he went up in the lift. Roper did not like working with beautiful women: he resented the energy it took to ignore their physical charms.

Dean's office was on the top floor, along with the executive boardroom. The Board of Directors met at the London building, where there were offices for those directors who wanted them. Roper had learned that the company was run by executives, rather than directors. The Board did pretty much what Dean and Shipley told them to. Sir Trevor Hollowood was the only full-time working director.

The Managing Director's room was L-shaped. One arm of the L contained a circle of club chairs and a coffee-table. When Roper entered, a group of executives was sitting around the table.

Dean walked across from his desk. "Ah, Piers," he said. "We have an informal meeting of senior executives on Friday afternoons. Review the week behind and the one ahead, you know. Coffee?"

Roper accepted a cup and took his seat. He recognised the other executives as Anthony Loughton, the Deputy Managing Director responsible for commercial vehicles; Inkleman, the Senior Production Executive; Giddins of Personnel; and Jones, the Research and Design boss. Sir Trevor came in to complete the team.

Dean sat down. He looked at Inkleman, the engineer. "Peter, shall we have the gearbox on the Capricorn sorted out next week?"

"I hope so." The man put down his coffee cup, blew his nose into a handkerchief, and stuffed it back into his breast pocket. "We're retooling over the weekend. It involves a design change in the selectors, and extra men on the production line. There's no foreseeable reason why the new parts shouldn't fit straight into the run on Monday morning."

"How much good will it do, Piers?" Roper thought rapidly. "I'm hoping it will make a significant difference," he said. "Dealers are making too little profit on Capricorns as it is. With so many coming back for gearbox work, they're better off shifting second-hand Cortinas." Piers knew that dealers got an allowance for warranty work which amply covered the minor repair job they were having to do on one in ten Capricorns: but the allowance was traditionally not spent, and it was universally reckoned part of the profit on a car. The free first service which a buyer was promised consisted of a few routine tightening-up jobs and a liberal use of oil to give the impression of a smoother-running car for a couple of days.

Piers added: "It will make a nice difference to the dealer's margin—which is not to say that the car will suddenly become vastly more attractive to customers."

Inkleman put in: "It's not an expensive modification, and the extra unit cost is fractional."

Dean said gruffly: "It still should have been done before we went on line with the damn car."

Anthony Loughton said: "The decision to hurry into production was a financial one, as I recall." He looked at Sir Trevor.

The Financial Director's face became angry; then he dropped his eyes. Piers watched the hidden clash with interest, and looked again at the smooth young deputy MD.

Dean gave Loughton a wary look. "We'd be a lot worse off if we'd postponed it," he said. He turned to Giddins. "I trust we'll have no union trouble over the retooling," he said.

The moment of tension had passed, but Piers had already sensed the strong undercurrents. He filed the incident in his memory.

It was late afternoon when the meeting broke up. Piers decided to set out for London. He picked up his briefcase, said good night to his secretary, and went down to Personnel. He put his head around the door and said: "Ready to leave, Miss Mainwaring?"

"You pronounced it wrongly again," she said. "I think you'd better call me Anne."

He carried her suitcase as they went down the stairs to the ground floor and out to the car park. She whistled when he stopped by the Bentley and put the case in its boot.

"Pullman class!" she said.

Piers drove out on to the main road and headed for the motorway. They were silent for a while. Eventually he said:

"Do you know why Sir Trevor Hollowood is frightened of Anthony Loughton?"

She raised her eyebrows. "I've no idea," she replied.

The following week Roper turned his attention to the commercial vehicle side of the Holmes Motor Corporation. Vans, lorries, coaches and buses were traditionally a pillar of strength in the company. Although it was Britain's third largest motor company overall, in the commercial field it was market leader. However, in the last three years English Motors Ltd.—the part-American-owned firm which had retained Palmer—had been catching up.

English Motors had bought up three small independent manufacturers with lucrative lines—one had a contract with the Army, another made single-decker coaches, a third specialised in dumper trucks. They had expanded their commercial operation and launched a well-designed range of vehicles based on a small number of interchangeable cabin and chassis units.

But it was not that which worried Roper. As he read on through the files and reports supplied to him by Laurence Dean, the picture which emerged became gloomier.

The basic problem seemed to be that Holmes' range of vehicles was very old. Five years ago they had introduced a completely new truck. A 30-cwt van, based on the same design principles, had been brought out a year later. Modifications and improvements had followed, and different sizes of truck and van launched. The operation had done well, and profits were still being made.

Sales had levelled out, but the profit margin on the vehicles was still high, because they had paid for their capital costs long ago. The range had years of profitable life left.

But that was not enough. To keep a hold on the market, a business had to do more than make a profit. Holmes should have brought out a basic new model at least a year ago. Roper determined to find out why they had not.

He told his secretary to get Anthony Loughton on the phone. A few moments later his intercom hummed. He pressed a key and said: "Loughton?"

His secretary's voice surprised him. "No, sir," she said. "He is at Moorville all day today."

"That's the test track, isn't it?"

"Yes."

Roper looked at his watch. It was mid-morning. "Get me a company car with a driver to take me out there." It was time he visited the track, anyway. "How far is it?"

"About thirty miles, I think."

"You'd better ring and let Mr. Loughton know I'm coming."

Five minutes later Roper was in the back of a company Diplomat being driven out of the works gate. It was an unpleasant April day, neither comfortably warm nor bitterly cold, and the rain dripped steadily from the grey sky. The big car pulled smoothly away down the road called Holmes Avenue. High chicken-wire fences closed off the auto factories along both sides of the road: the body shop, the upholstery plant, the electrical works, and the massive production line itself. It was a higgledy-piggledy assortment of buildings which had been bought, built, altered and extended over many years. For all their diverse shapes and sizes they had one thing in common: a thick, oily layer of grime which the heaviest rainfall did nothing to shift.

The car sped on, past the city boundaries, through traffic-battered suburbs where 1930s semi-detached dream homes were on the way to becoming decayed slums, out into open country. Roper wound the window down a millimetre to let in the air of raw ploughed fields and new leaves.

The test track was five miles of disused airstrip more heavily guarded than Buckingham Palace. Both Roper and his driver had to show pink plasticised identity cards to the security men at the entrance gate, who then insisted on looking in the boot of the car before letting them in.

The Diplomat pulled up beside a row of cars near a wide, low building. Roper told his driver to go and find himself a cup of tea. Then he got out of the car. The wind gusted across the flat landscape, driving the rain before it. Roper hurried across the tarmac to the building.

He found Anthony Loughton at the far side of the building, which was an aeroplane hangar converted into a workshop. The Deputy Managing Director was at the workshop entrance, his head under the bonnet of a car. He wore a quilted black anorak with a red stripe down the sleeve, and was surrounded by mechanics.

Loughton looked up. "Ah, Roper," he said. "Got your message." He did not seem very happy to see Roper. He turned back and spoke to the mechanics, then he and Piers walked away from the car. "I suppose you'd like to look around?"

"Please," Piers replied. "I've been studying our performance in the commercial field and I'd like to see what we've got coming up."

"Sure, sure." Loughton took a pipe from his anorak pocket and began to fill it. Piers thought the pipe oddly out of character.

"Well, we've got two commercial variations of the Capricorn which will be in production very soon," Loughton began. He led Piers over to the far side of the hangar and pointed to a very dirty van with a broken headlamp. "This is the 15 cwt.," he went on. "It's a Capricorn Estate without windows or back seats. It has a version of the 1600 engine from the Capricorn Coupé, and slightly modified rear suspension to improve its load-bearing capacity."

He walked on a few yards to where a shiny Diplomat stood in stately contrast to the lower-class van. "This is an idea of my own," he said. "It's basically an underpowered Diplomat. The car is impressive, roomy, has lots of boot space, and is economical." He paused.

Roper said: "So who will buy it?"

"Small taxi firms," Loughton replied triumphantly. "The customers like an impressive car when they order a taxi. They also need lots of space. But they aren't going very far, so they don't need speed. And the driver likes the economy."

"It's a good idea," Piers said. "We'll have to run a special marketing operation on it."

"Splendid," Loughton announced. "Now there's another Capricorn somewhere which is converted for use as an open pick-up." He looked around the vast workshop.

Piers said: "Tell me, Loughton, why is it so long since we brought out a brand-new truck?"

Loughton looked at him sharply. "A good question," he said, "and there's a good answer. Come this way."

He led Piers through a steel door in the brick hangar wall, across a muddy lawn, and into a smaller building. They both had to show their pink passes again at the door.

"We have a new lorry which is scheduled to go on line in seven or eight months," he said as they walked. "You're right —it has been too long since we brought out a new range. This is the reason."

They had stopped in front of what seemed to be an ordinary three-ton rigid truck. Loughton continued: "It's part of a whole range. There's a single cab unit which fits any vehicle from the 30-cwt. van to the juggernaut. Every truck in the range has more volume than any comparable lorry of the same weight. The thing is packed with revolutionary design features, from the bumpers to the tailgate. But the best of it is the suspension. You'll have to ask Jones for the technical details, but I can tell you this: the load-bearing capacity is *thirty-three per cent* better than anything the opposition can offer."

He patted the cab door affectionately. "This one is going to sweep the board for us, Roper."

The crisis began to turn into a disaster on Tuesday, when English Motors announced their Diamond.

Roper read about it in The Times as he sat in the back of the company car which took him from his hotel to the office in the morning. The management of Holmes had known a new car was coming from English; and it was general knowledge within the industry that it would-be a medium-priced family saloon. But nobody was prepared for the Diamond.

For a start, it looked terrific. It was sleek and graceful, in contrast to the rather businesslike blunt-ended appearance of the Capricorn and similar cars. It boasted a whole series of design innovations under the bonnet, and it matched American safety regulations. And it cost £49 less than the Capricorn.

The motoring writers were ecstatic. The Times man had the perspicacity to note that this was the first completely new car English had produced since the Americans had bought into the company.

Roper ran over the implications in his mind while he drove to the office. When he got in he rang Holmes' advertising agency in London and spoke to its chief.

He spoke without preamble. "Mr. Leon, we haven't met but you'll know I'm the new Senior Marketing Executive at Holmes."

The man began to utter some pleasantry, but Piers cut him off abruptly. Any minute now he would be summoned to Dean's office. "I'd like to see you this weekend. I'll be in town.

"We must have a new advertising campaign for the Capricorn, and fast. You'll have read about English Motors' Diamond in the papers. It's going to take a lot of beating.

"I want you to come equipped with some ideas. I want to see a really strong campaign. I think the idea to emphasise will be that the Capricorn is a simple car: no spare tin to make it look faster, no fancy engineering to bring high repair bills—that sort of thing."

Leon said: "I'll get a team on it this morning."

"Good. I will get in touch again and arrange for us to meet." Piers hung up. There was no question that the agency boss would cancel any other weekend arrangements he had in order to see Piers. Accounts like Holmes' were hard to come by, and the loss of one would be near fatal to any but the biggest agency.

Roper looked at his watch. It was 9.25, and Dean arrived at 9.30. There was time for one more call. He rang his Sales Executive.

"Arrange a conference of reps in London on Saturday. Book a hotel. The purpose of the meeting is to discuss our strategy for beating the Diamond. I want every rep there." He hung up without waiting for a reply.

As he rested the handset in its cradle his secretary came on the intercom. "Mr. Dean would like to see you in his office right away, please," she said. The urgency had already got through to her, Piers could tell. He went out.

The atmosphere in Dean's room was very different to what it had been the previous Friday. There was no coffee, no idle chatter. The company's top executives sat around on the armchairs, looking clean-shaven and early-morningish.

Roper sat down and took a Senior Service from his case. Evan Jones, the Design Chief, was speaking.

"Ninety per cent of these features are on the drawing boards for the BX Two," he said. Roper remember that the BX Two was the planned successor to the Capricorn. "They are just a couple of years ahead of us. They must have spent millions on research to get this far already."

Dean looked at Roper and said: "No matter how they've done it. We're in trouble now. Piers, all talk of letting you feel your way around for a while stops here. You're in at the deep end. This is a marketing problem now."

Roper looked around at the group, then let his eyes return to the Managing Director. "For the immediate future, I've done two things. We're working on a new advertising campaign. It's time to take the gloves off in our ads, and our agency is setting up the theme of the Capricorn as the sensible

74

car: no gimmicky engineering, no flashy bits of styling, but the kind of car that the intelligent man goes for in the end.

"I've also set up a pep-talk for reps this weekend. But this is just a start. We need a new car, and we can't produce one out of a hat. Therefore the Capricorn must become a new car.

"What I'm suggesting is that we bring out a Mark Two Capricorn in October. It will look slightly different, incorporate whatever we can learn from the Diamond, and—most important—have a new image."

Dean looked questioningly at Inkleman, the Senior Production Executive.

"It could certainly be done," the man said. "We'll start thinking about the details."

"This is all very well," put in Sir Trevor Hollowood. "But however much we put into this campaign it remains a defensive operation. We live or die by margins, as you well know; and the Diamond is certain to shave a margin off the Capricorn. That margin is probably a year or two's profit on the car.

"We have to put that profit back into the company somehow. At the moment our only hope seems to be Anthony's new truck."

Dean nodded, then looked at Anthony Loughton. "It seems the life or death of this company now rests with that lorry," he said grimly.

Roper sat back on the angular modern arm-chair in his hotel suite and breathed a long relieved sigh. It had been a hard day. He had spent most of the previous night with the team from the advertising agency, hammering out the details of the campaign. They had decided on a series of ads around the slogan "No Clever Stuff". Each advert would carry a different sub-heading emphasising some aspect of the Capricorn: one was "Just sound British engineering"; another "Just value for your money".

He had snatched a few hours' sleep around dawn and got up

to spend the day with the men who sold Capricorn to car dealers. They had been told of the high-powered national media campaign which was to back them up over the crucial months ahead, and they had been given some idea of the plans for a Mark Two Capricorn in the autumn.

A couple of hours ago the salesmen had been set loose on London to finish off their Saturday with a binge. The executives who had run the conference had gathered in the lounge of Roper's suite at the hotel for de-briefing and drinks.

Piers decided the discussion was tailing off into trivia. "Gentlemen, I think we've covered the ground," he said. He put down his glass and stood up. As the others stood he said: "Oh, Miss Mainwaring, would you look out the North-East figures for me before you go?"

The men trooped out. Roper watched the Personnel Officer hunt through a file for a set of figures he knew were not there. Her flame-coloured dress swung attractively about her knees as she walked across the room, an exasperated frown on her face. She began looking at another file. A multi-coloured silk scarf which matched the dress had worked a little loose at her neck. The bold colour of her clothes might have looked tarty, but she had enough natural poise to carry it off.

He went to the mobile bar and poured another drink for each of them. He took hers to her. As he handed it over she said, absent-mindedly: "You still mispronounce my name. Why don't you call me Annie?"

"It doesn't suit you," he replied. "It's such an unglamorous name."

She looked at him, slightly surprised. She seemed about to say something, then turned her attention to the file.

He put his hands to her neck and adjusted the scarf so that it sat firmly on her throat. "You've been a great help today," he told her. "Thank you."

She seemed slightly flustered. "I'm afraid I can't find these figures."

76

"Leave it. It's getting too late to bother with them now. Drink your drink."

She sat down on a wide sofa. Beside her was a table with a cigarette box. She flipped the lid open and took one. Roper sat down beside her.

He said: "How long have you been divorced?"

"How did you know?"

"It's no secret."

"Ten years."

Piers upped his estimate of her age again.

"Mid-thirties," she offered.

"What?"

"You were figuring out my age. Wasn't that the point of the question?"

"Good Lord, no."

She laughed her deep chuckle, and Piers found himself looking too hard at the line of her throat as she threw her head back.

"Any children?" he said.

"No, thank God. A nice, clean break. No mess, no alimony."

"And no regrets," Piers supplied.

"What makes you so sure?"

"You've done well, haven't you? There can't be many women in their mid-thirties who earn as much as you do."

She walked to the big french window that led on to the balcony. "I didn't realise you could see the river from here," she said.

Piers opened the windows and stepped out. The night air was cold and dry. Anne came to his side.

"It takes a long time to get rid of the feeling of failure," she said quietly. She fiddled with her scarf.

"Let me," said Piers, and rearranged it for the second time.

"Does the scarf fascinate you?"

"No," he said in a low voice. "The throat does." He untied it, leaned forward, and bent his head to kiss her neck. Then he

77

kissed her lips.

She put her arms around his waist and leaned back to look at him. "What fun it would be to walk out on the calculating Mr. Roper," she said.

"Why?"

"Just to show you that human individuals can't be manipulated quite as easily as mass markets. Besides, it would be prudent."

"So what's keeping you here?"

"You've got a rather tight grip on me, for one thing." She stood on tiptoe and kissed him again.

Then she said into his ear: "And for another, I'm curious to know what happens when the ice melts."

He bent down, put an arm under her thighs, lifted her, and carried her through the hotel suite to the bedroom. There he unzipped her dress and slid it over her shoulders. She dug her fingers into the muscles of his thighs. "What a fit 41-year-old you are," she murmured.

"And what a facetious lover you are!" he replied.

She undid his trousers and let them fall to the carpet. Then she leaned against him, with her eyes half closed, pressing her soft belly against his hips. "I don't believe sex ought to be too solemn," she said. "And you're solemn about everything, aren't you?"

He brushed his lips across the top of her head as she nuzzled into his chest. Suddenly she pulled away from him and said: "Take off your clothes, quickly."

When they lay naked on the bed she crushed his body to her and said: "Piers, you bastard, I don't need you. Why do I want you?"

He took her small nipple between his lips and teased it with his tongue. He rubbed the heel of his hand slowly to and fro across her pubis. Eventually he mounted her, and she gave a long sigh of satisfaction when she felt him inside her. She gripped his buttocks and controlled the movement of his hips

78

with her hands, pulling him to her harder and faster, until she came with a series of hoarse gasps.

"Thank you, Piers," she said as he rolled off her. He fumbled for a cigarette in the heap of clothes on the floor. When he had it alight, he passed it to her and she drew on it gratefully.

"Is your curiosity satisfied?" he asked her.

She chuckled, it seemed even more deeply than usual. "Of course not," she said. "The ice didn't melt, did it?" She sucked on the cigarette again and passed it back to him. "But it will," she added.

She got up off the bed and started to climb into her clothes. "Are you going to explain that?" Piers asked her.

She knotted her scarf and found a comb in her handbag. "I'm sure you know what I mean." She looked in the mirror, then replaced the comb in her handbag. Piers wrapped a dressing-gown around himself. Anne said: "As a lover, you're dull and mechanical. But you've got enormous potential."

"How disarmingly candid," Piers said.

He went to the bedroom door with her. "Will you be my Personnel Officer for a minute before you go?" he said.

"All right."

"Have you ever come across a foundry worker called Briggs?"

"Yes," she said straight away. "He's a supervisor. I know the name because he runs a pools syndicate. They won some money a couple of months ago, and it was in the house magazine."

"I thought I'd seen the name," he said. "Fine. Now stop being my Personnel Officer and kiss me good night."

He kissed her lips, gently. She said: "I like you, Piers." Then she turned and walked quickly away.

When the door closed Roper said: "My God."

He walked back into the bedroom and took off his gown. The woman baffled him. But more important was what she had said about Briggs. A pools syndicate! That gave him a reason for going anywhere in the plant, contacting staff from any department. And now Piers could find out who his agents were.

It had been a good evening's work. He got into bed and turned off the light.

# Five

The grey sky was dusted with pink as the sun set over Hertford-
shire. The Bentley was doing 100 mph down the M1, and
Roper knew it. He had a feeling that his quite unnecessary
speeding had something to do with the fact that Anne Mainwaring was his passenger, but he did not try to analyse his
motivation. He was enjoying it.

He had spent most of the journey telling her anecdotes about
army life. He did not normally enjoy reminiscing about his
National Service; but he did it now for the sheer pleasure of
hearing Anne's delicious, lusty laugh.

"You had a very funny army career, for such a humourless
man," she said finally. He was getting used to the way she
sprinkled her conversation with derogatory remarks.

"Now why do you think I'm humourless?" he said with an
indulgent smile.

"Piers, you really don't know yourself, do you. I don't think
I've ever heard you actually laugh, and a smile is as rare as a
waterfall in Palestine."

"So I don't know myself."

"No." Her tone became exhortatory, as if she were making
a point in a political debate. "You're blind to your faults.
You're conceited, arrogant, manipulative and incredibly
smug."

"Thank you," he said.

"Oh, now you're playing injured pride." She leaned across
and put her hand on his stomach, under his jacket. She laid
her head on his shoulder and watched the road in front. "It
must be because you have virtually no emotional life," she

went on in a reflective voice. "Your personality has been moulded entirely by your working environment, where energy and poise count, and compassion is a low-profit enterprise."

He spoke brightly, as if he had not heard her. "Have you got any plans for the weekend?"

"Yes," she said.

"Oh," he said expressionlessly.

"Why?"

"I was hoping you might spend a dirty weekend at my flat."

"But that's just what my plans are."

He looked down at her in surprise, and she chuckled again.

Roper hurried through North London and along the Edgware Road, shooting the lights and accelerating too hard. The worst of the rush-hour traffic had dispersed, and they reached Marble Arch quickly.

"We'll eat before we go home, shall we?" Piers suggested. She agreed, and he pointed the car towards Chelsea.

He took her to a basement restaurant in a cul-de-sac off the King's Road, where she polished off a huge steak and a jacket potato while he toyed with breast of turkey and green salad. They drank a bottle of burgundy.

She looked mockingly at him over the oil lamp which burned smokily in the centre of their table. "You seem nervous," she said.

He put down his fork. "And you seem too damn perceptive," he said. He emptied his wineglass. "I'm just wondering how not to be dull and mechanical," he said. His own words surprised him. Her ruthless honesty seemed to be contagious.

"Don't let it trouble you," she said. "Tonight I'm running the show."

Roper felt perfectly sober when they left the restaurant, but he drove home fairly slowly just the same, knowing that his apparent sobriety would not impress a breathalyser bag if he happened to be involved in an accident.

He parked in the road outside the house and carried her suitcase up the stairs to his flat. He showed her into one of the two spare bedrooms, and pointed to a door leading off it. "Since we've got two bathrooms we might as well use both," he said.

He left her to change and went into his own bedroom. He showered quickly and dressed again in black trousers, white shirt, grey jacket and black tie. Then he went into the drawing-room and made up two drinks.

She came in a few minutes later. Her denim jeans fitted very tightly around her hips and thighs, then dangled loosely about her bare feet. She wore a soft woollen sweater which ended an inch short of the tooled leather belt in her jeans. Piers noticed she had rewritten her face, making it up to look less formal: but her beautiful eyes seemed even wider. She looked at Piers' clothes and said: "My God, is that what you wear for loafing around the house?"

He handed her a drink in a heavy, squat glass. "I never loaf, anywhere," he replied.

She swirled the whisky around the glass. The ice touched the edges with a dull knocking sound instead of a high-pitched chink. "I like your glasses," she said. Then she swallowed the drink in one gulp. "But I can see it will take more than whisky to break down your inhibitions."

She took his glass out of his hand and put them both on the floor. Then she knelt astride him on the settee. She kissed his forehead, then her lips moved all over his face, nibbling and biting his chin, his eyelids, and his cheeks. He closed his eyes and enjoyed the sensation: she was like a butterfly flitting from place to place on his skin. She sucked at his upper lip, then the lower one, and finally her tongue pushed inside his mouth.

His lips felt the fine, invisible border of hair along her upper lip. He stroked the rough denim along her flanks, then raised his hands under her sweater and felt the warmth of her skin. He ran his fingertips around her ribs to her breasts, and dis-

83

covered with a shock of pleasure that she had taken off her brassiere. His hands completely enclosed the small, pointed breasts.

He felt her undo his tie and the buttons of his shirt. She pushed jacket, shirt and tie aside and ran her hands lustfully across his chest. She rubbed his nipples with the palms of her hands. He opened his eyes in surprise, expecting to see her grinning her mocking grin at him; but her eyes were shut and her face bore the languid look of a woman who is engrossed in a sensation.

Her lips tracked down his neck, along his shoulder, and down to his chest. He felt as if he was being ravished, and was slightly horrified to find he liked it. She sucked his nipple. It was deliciously improper, almost perverted. He gave a pleasured sigh which turned inexplicably into a grunt of satisfaction.

She undid his trousers. Without thinking he raised himself for her to pull them off. He was astonished at how easily the gesture came. Somehow his pants came off too, then his shoes and socks. Anne stood up and looked at him. He should have been embarrassed, but he just smiled. She pulled her sweater over her head. They looked at each other's half-naked bodies for a moment. Piers went to take off his jacket, but she stopped him. "It's more fun with some clothes on," she murmured.

He slouched in the seat. The pile of the upholstery felt oddly pleasant to his bare skin. Anne lay on top of him. Her busy lips trailed across his hard, flat stomach.

He pressed her head into his body, stroking her short, fine hair. For the first time he noticed the dark brown head had auburn lights which gleamed when they caught the glow from the lamps in the room.

The sensations from his loins filled his head and excluded all thought. He reached down to her shoulders and pulled her hard against him. He began to move slowly, helplessly, as the familiar knot of pleasure tightened.

Her soft breasts caressed his skin like a mild electric shock.

Her breath was hot on his stomach and she sighed heavily. He arched his body, and the sensation destroyed his self-control. He crushed her brutally to him.

He felt the sudden build-up of pressure and realised—too late—that he had lost control. Every muscle tightened as the last spasm came: then he fell back.

He lay there for a moment, his arms and legs spread wide and his head thrown back, taking in deep draughts of air. Then he opened his eyes and saw her looking into his face.

She said: "Don't look so guilty? You look like a small boy caught raiding the pantry."

He stroked her cheek with his long fingers and smiled weakly. "I found some sensational goodies there, but I forgot to leave some for my friend," he said.

She took his hand. "What makes you think they're all gone?" she said in a husky voice. "Come to the shower with me." She pulled him up.

He left the rest of his clothes behind and followed her out of the room, across the hall, through his bedroom and into the bathroom. She stopped in the doorway and pushed down her jeans. Piers felt a throb of desire stir as she bent over to slip the garment off her feet.

He pulled the light cord, and the sudden brightness reflecting off the white tiles hurt his eyes. He turned on the water and they both stepped into the shower cubicle. She handed him the soap and said: "You wash me."

The faint scent of the soap rose to his nostrils as he rubbed the smooth lather over her tanned body. He soaped her neck and shoulders, then her breasts. They were still taut with desire, and the film of soap over the skin made them feel delightfully slippery. He worked across the slight bulge of her belly. She leaned against him.

He pushed his fingers underneath her. "That's nice," she breathed.

After a moment she lifted her face up into the stream of hot

85

water. She took the soap from him. "Now it's your turn," she said.

She soaped his belly and his thighs. He felt himself unfold with desire again, and was amazed at the soonness of it.

Suddenly she stood up and leaned against the wall. Drops of water glittered on the tiles and on her hair. She pulled him to her. He lowered himself by spreading his legs wide, until their hips were level. Her eyes were closed and her mouth wide open. She breathed in quick pants, almost sobs. He put his hands behind her, as she strained against him. Suddenly she cried: "Aah!" several times and bared her teeth in a savage grin of passion. They thrust at one another in short, ecstatic jerks, and climaxed helplessly.

Piers got his breath back in a series of ragged gasps. He switched off the shower. Suddenly his legs felt weak. "Bed," he said.

They did not bother to dry themselves, but fell between the sheets and lay there exhausted.

"You see?" said Anne after a while. "I told you you had potential."

Piers sighed contentedly.

She threw back the sheet. She kissed him gently.

Incredibly, Piers felt aroused again. She looked up at him, and he thought how good the brownness of her hair and eyes looked against the pale blue sheet.

"Christ," he murmured.

There were no preliminaries this time. He rolled on top of her and thrust himself inside her. They moved savagely and quickly now, like animals, shouting coarse words at one another. Anne built quickly to her climax, panting for air. Then her words slurred into a shout of joy. The burning pleasure spread suddenly. Anne's legs locked about his waist, squeezing like a vice. She heaved helplessly as the orgasm shook her. Piers' orgasm was almost painful, as if he were being wrung out.

He rolled off her.

"It's strange, you know," she said.

His eyes closed and he felt an irresistible desire to sleep. "What is?" he mumbled.

"You don't usually swear," she replied.

But he was asleep before she finished the sentence.

Piers woke instantly at the touch on his shoulder. Anne stood beside the bed. She was dressed in her jeans and nothing else, and her breasts swung freely as she bent to kiss him.

"You look sensational," he said sleepily, and stretched.

She had set a tea-tray on the bedside-table, and she turned to it and poured. Piers sat up in bed and reached for the cigarettes.

He sucked on a Senior Service and rode the kick it gave him. Then he sipped at the tea. The hot liquid sluiced away the gummy taste of a night's sleep.

The details of the night before came back to him. He laid his hand on hers. "You were m-m-marvellous," he stammered.

She frowned. "My God, it costs you that much to say it," she said, almost to herself. Then she smiled at him. "You were pretty phenomenal yourself, for a man who's led a sheltered life," she said.

"Not so sheltered."

"No." She took one of his cigarettes and lit it. "Why do you smoke these? The bits get in my mouth."

"Twenty-five years of ingrained habit."

"You've had other women," she mused. "But somehow you've dominated them, so that they only gave what you asked for. And you didn't have the imagination to experiment with them."

She was getting uncomfortably close to the truth. Piers crushed out his cigarette and threw the bedclothes aside. He leaned over to where she sat on the edge of the bed and kissed her breasts.

87

"No," he said firmly. "Not this early." He jumped out of bed and strode to the bathroom.

As he shaved he contemplated the effect Anne was having on him. He had intended to seduce her in order to get her into his power. He needed access to the Personnel files at Holmes' and if she was besotted with him she would not question him too closely. But he had obviously misjudged her. She would never be dominated by any man, he guessed. That meant he had to find some other way of getting at the files. But that was a lesser problem.

As soon as he knew she was going to be no use he should have dropped her. He still could do that, if he wanted to. The trouble was he did not want to.

Quite the contrary.

He had always taken pleasure in sex with beautiful women, although lately he found he wanted it less and less. But pleasure was one thing: the kind of devastating ecstasy he had experienced with Anne was something else. He felt he had just found out what it was all about—and he knew he was not going to give it up straight away.

He finished shaving and patted his face dry with a hot towel. In the bedroom, Anne sat and watched him dress.

"You've a lot of wardrobe space for one person," she remarked

"Not really," he said. There were two double wardrobes along one wall of the bedroom. He pointed to them. "One for jackets, the other for shirts."

She walked over and opened one. "Piers!" she exclaimed. "There must be forty identical white shirts in here!"

He grinned. "The rest are at the laundry," he said.

"Do you know, that's the first time I've heard you crack a joke," she said.

"I don't like coloured shirts," Piers added.

She continued her inspection. "Six pairs of black brogues, all the same," she said faintly. She opened a drawer. "Innumerable black socks. Dozens of pairs of black underpants. Fifteen or twenty black knitted ties, all ten years out of fashion. A wardrobe full of dark suits. A whole drawer full of white handkerchiefs, although I've never seen you use one. Oho!"

He looked around. She was holding up a pair of white frilly knickers.

"So you have had other women," she said.

He knotted his tie. "Yes. Have you?"

"I've never had other women. I'm not sure I'd like it. Still, you never know."

"You can't be serious."

"Why not?"

He shook his head in bewilderment. "I've never met a woman like you," he said.

"Show me around your flat," she demanded. She pointed to the door opposite. "What's in there—more shirts?"

He walked over and opened the door. "The gym," he said. She went in. "Wow!" she exclaimed. "Do you use it?"

"Of course. At my age . . ."

She hugged him impulsively. "For your age, you're pretty young," she said.

He kissed the top of her head. "It's thanks to you, not the gym, if I am," he whispered.

She pulled away. "Come on, show me the rest."

He led her back through the bedroom and into the hall. "As we walk towards the front door, you see the bedrooms on your right," he said. "First the master bedroom, which we've just left. The next door leads to my bathroom. Two more doors for two more bedrooms, then the cloakroom. Turning back, we now have on our right the drawing-room and the dining-room. At the end of the hall, opposite the front door, is the kitchen."

As he pointed out the rooms she opened the heavy black doors and peeped in. Eventually they stopped in the kitchen. "You keep the place spotlessly clean," she said.

"Not I—Mrs. Cooper," he said. "She does the cleaning, takes stuff to the laundry, shops, and washes up."

"Doesn't she cook for you?"

"Ah. That's where you underestimate me." He took a big saucepan from a wall cupboard and set about making porridge.

"I never eat breakfast," she protested.

"You should," was all he would say.

He put the pan of water on the cooker and stirred in oats from a cardboard packet. She sat at the bleached pine table, her arms folded under her bare breasts, and watched him. He kept stealing glances at her.

"Look," he said when the porridge was bubbling. "You look very beautiful dressed like that, but is it suitable for breakfast-time?"

"I'll change," she laughed. "How long have I got?"

"Four and a half minutes," he told her.

She came back, in a knee-length flared skirt and a shirt, as he was spooning the porridge into two stoneware bowls. She sat down and tasted. "I did underestimate you," she said. "I never thought something as mundane as porridge could taste so delicious."

"Then I've returned the favour," he murmured, half under his breath. The look she gave him was knowing. She seemed about to say something, but changed her mind and returned to her breakfast.

"Well, what shall we do with the day?" Piers asked her when she had finished.

"Make love?"

"I mean, what else."

"Mmmm." She looked out of the window. "We ought to spend some time under that beautiful blue sky."

"Then we shall." He got up and loaded the dishes into the dishwashing machine.

"I thought you said Mrs. Cooper did the washing-up."

"Well, she puts the dishes in here and switches it on."

"It must be an easy life, being your char."

"Want the job? You're much more decorative than Mrs. Cooper, even with your clothes on."

"No thanks. You're too much of a perfectionist. I couldn't stand the strain."

Piers put on a jacket and they went out into the sunshine. The sky was a startling shade of picture-postcard blue, scarred with the white trails of jet aircraft. A warm breeze stirred the air, and the sun beat hotly down on the pavements.

They walked up to Hyde Park Corner and crossed the road. When they entered the park, Piers took Anne's hand. She gave him a swift glance which he could not read, then squeezed his fingers.

Piers thought that a man of his age probably looked slightly undignified, walking in the park hand-in-hand with a girl. Somehow the thought did not bother him. He felt contented—too contented to puzzle over the reason for the way he felt. He talked to Anne in a quiet voice about trivia, and found himself taking an interest in mundane things like the bright green colour of new leaves and the wrinkled parchment of an old man's face.

They came out at Speakers' Corner, and bought cans of Coca-Cola at grossly inflated prices from a hot-dog stall. While they sipped the soft drinks through straws, they listened to a tall, handsome black man haranguing a little crowd. He was talking about police brutality in Brixton.

"Lot of rubbish," said Piers as they moved away. "But he has a great future as a salesman."

Anne took his empty can and dropped it in a litter bin along with her own. "What would you know about it?" she said.

"I'm a salesman myself, remember? That chap has—"

"No, I mean what would you know about the way the police treat black people."

"The same way they treat everyone else, I'm sure."

"How can an intelligent man get to your age and be so

ignorant?"

Piers frowned. "Surely you don't believe all that stuff about beatings-up, faked charges . . ."

"I'm sure he knows more about it than you do."

"I suppose he does. Let's walk down Oxford Street."

They strolled, still hand-in-hand, looking in shop windows and enjoying the feeling of nothing to do. "Tell me how you came to be a high-ranking executive in a leading motor company," Piers asked her.

"Well, I married a handsome, charming man who was terrific in bed and had strong ideas about the man being master in the house, so I divorced him," she replied. "That left me with some capital so I started an accommodation agency. I built it up until it was worth a great deal of money, then sold it and got a job with Holmes. What about you?"

"Oh, it was just another step up the ladder," he said. They came to Oxford Circus and turned into Regent Street. "Shall we have some coffee soon?"

"Please."

They turned down a side street and went into a wood-fronted shop with tiny windows. Piers ordered coffee and cream cakes.

"You know what interpretation would be put on this if we were seen together?" Anne said.

"Tell me."

"People would jump to the conclusion I reached the first time you offered me a lift."

Suddenly Piers' interest quickened. "Which was?"

"That you wanted to use me to get at my boss, Mr. Giddins. To find out something to discredit him."

Piers disguised his feeling of relief. She had not been perceptive enough to guess his true motive. "And why would I want to discredit Giddins?" he said. "He's harmless enough."

"Just to score a point for your side in the boardroom."

"Wait a minute, you're losing me. There's supposed to be

some boardroom battle in which Giddins and I are on separate sides?"

Her face darkened. "I'm sorry," she said. "I forgot myself. You can't discuss these things with a subordinate, of course." The coffee arrived and she stirred sugar into hers.

"Don't be so silly," he said gently. "I'm not dissembling. Now let me see. Is the battle supposed to be over something to do with Personnel?"

She raised her eyebrows. "Do you really not know?"

"Really not. Have a cream cake."

She selected a meringue and dug into it with a fork. "Delicious. It's about the Americans, of course."

"Ah. That figures. One side wants a merger with an American motor company, the other is resisting it."

"So I heard."

"Let me guess some more. The anti-American faction is led by Dean, Lord Shipley, and Sir Trevor Hollowood. Giddins is on the other side, and I'm supposed to be with the Dean faction."

"Don't tell me you just guessed all that."

"It wasn't difficult. I was recruited by Dean, Shipley and Hollowood. They asked me some peculiar questions about the Americans. This explains it."

"Aren't you having a cream cake?"

"No thank you. There's no quicker way to a heart attack than cream cakes."

She laughed, and rummaged in her bag for cigarettes. When she had one in her mouth Piers lit it. He watched her for a moment.

"Why did I think your eyes were green?" he said.

"What do you mean?"

"I thought your eyes were green when I first met you. I actually noticed the colour. But they're brown."

"I think you're colour blind."

"It must be the eye shadow." He lifted a finger at a waitress, and she brought the bill.

They finished their cigarettes and left. As they walked south down Regent Street, Anne said: "Tonight I want to take you to a concert. I have tickets."

"Good."

They paused at the window of a jeweller's, and Piers pointed to a ladies' wristwatch. "It's beautiful," Anne agreed. Its tiny face was set in a wide gold strap, and the price was £367.50. They walked on, and she insisted they go inside Austin Reed.

"I stopped buying clothes here when they went fashion-conscious," Piers protested.

She picked out a red shirt with a high collar. Piers grimaced.

"I'm going to buy it for you, whether you like it or not," she said with a mischievous grin. She paid for it and the assistant went to wrap it up. "You'll look terrific in it," she went on.

"I shall never wear it in public," he warned.

"It can be your screwing shirt," she giggled.

"Hush!" He looked around, but there was no one near enough to hear.


"Is this concert formal?" Piers called out.

Anne replied from the bathroom where she lay in the bath, smoking. "Quite the contrary," she said.

Piers unpacked the shirt she had bought him. He did not like it. Wearing white shirts was one of the unquestioned rules of life for him: like voting Conservative, smoking Senior Service, and not talking to small children. But he wanted very much to please Anne. He methodically removed the pins, plastic clips, and cardboard stiffeners from the shirt and shook it out.

Anne stopped singing The Birth of the Blues and started on Doctor Jazz. Piers put the red shirt on, chafing at the new stiffness of the cotton on his neck. He shouted: "Who are we going to hear, anyway?"

She interrupted her singing to say: "The Mahavishnu Orchestra."

"Oh dear," Piers said. "Is that a cover name for the Rangoon Philharmonic, or something?"

"Wait and see," she replied. "The more I get the more I want it seems," she sang. "I page old Doctor Jazz in all my dreams." She forgot the words and began to scat. There was a lot of splashing about, then the plug came out.

Piers selected his most modern suit, a grey lightweight made of Swedish cloth with lapels half an inch broader than he normally wore. He put on one of his black ties and examined the result in the full-length mirror inside the wardrobe door.

"Piers, you're wearing it," her voice came from the doorway. She was wrapped in a huge white towel.

"Just for you," he replied.

She came close and stood on tiptoe to kiss him. "But it doesn't look right," she said.

"I could have predicted that."

"Look." She pointed him at the mirror. "It has a high collar, with long points. You can't wear a thin tie with it."

"I have no wide ties."

She undid his tie, took it off, and unbuttoned the collar. "See how the top front button is set high, just under the collar button? That's so it can be worn without a tie. Now. Doesn't that look better?"

Piers studied the effect in the mirror. "Fine, for a male model perhaps. Really, you don't want me to go to a concert without a tie?"

"You look so appetising like that," she pleaded.

Piers shook his head in mock bewilderment. "I just hope I don't see anyone I know."

"I don't think you will," she replied with a secretive smile. She dropped the bath towel and opened her suitcase, taking out clean underwear. Piers watched as she put on her brassiere first: she looked very sexy in a bra and no knickers. He

95

wondered whether she dressed in that order for effect. He tore his eyes away. He went over to the open window and sniffed the air.

"Still very warm," he remarked. "We shan't need coats."

He went into the drawing-room, made two drinks, and brought them back into the bedroom. She was pulling on her stockings.

"I thought all women wore tights now," he commented.

"Not for dirty weekends with men who remember the first edition of Playboy."

"I don't remember any edition of Playboy."

"No, but you're old enough to. I suppose when you were a teenager you used to have a torch under the sheets at night and read The Economist."

"Investors' Chronicle, actually."

She looked at him wide-eyed.

He laughed. "You'd believe that of me, wouldn't you."

"Take it easy. I'm supposed to be the mickey-taker around here."

She finished dressing and swallowed her drink. She took Piers' hand and looked at his wristwatch. "Let's go," she said. "We'll be late."

As he opened the front door she stopped him, stood back and examined him. He noticed that she had altered her eye make-up again, and now her eyes looked green.

"Piers, you look literally edible," she said.

They went out into the street and hailed a cab. Anne gave the driver the name of a concert hall.

"Do you get that Saturday-night-out feeling?" she said as they sat in the moving taxi. "You know, when you're all dressed-up and on your way somewhere to enjoy yourself?"

"I know the feeling," he replied. "But I get it when you start to undress."

She giggled and hugged him. It was amazing, he reflected, how she managed to combine cynicism, sexual sophistication,

96

and a hard-headed intelligence with such a fresh, wide-eyed delight in simple pleasures.

The cab decanted them on the South Bank, and they went in to the concert hall. As Anne handed over the tickets in the foyer, Piers noticed that the audience streaming in was mostly young, and the sprinkling of older people tended to have youthful clothes and hair. Perhaps he had been right not to wear a tie. Dressed as he was, he still looked rather formal in this milieu.

When they took their seats Piers looked at the stage in puzzlement. There was a set of drums, some kind of electric organ, a few microphones and banks of loudspeakers.

"It's a wretched pop group!" he whispered to Anne in horror.

She chuckled. "Right first time."

"Oh my God."

The audience burst into applause as the group ambled on to the stage. Two carried guitars, and one a violin. A negro sat at the drums. The fifth shifted a microphone nearer to the organ. Piers settled back to endure the torture.

The drummer struck up a rapid, complex tattoo, and the music started. Piers found it painfully loud. The violinist and the first guitarist played together, very fast, and he found himself admiring the sheer speed at which they moved their fingers. He was surprised that there was no singing.

In between numbers, the first guitarist mumbled incomprehensibly into the microphone. Gradually Piers realised he had been wrong to dismiss them as a wretched pop group. He began to see what they were trying to do with their music. The violinist's tone would have got him sacked from a grammar school orchestra, but it was plainly wrong to judge him on that basis: as wrong as evaluating an opera purely on its plot.

By the time the concert ended Piers was getting quite interested. As they left their seats he said to Anne: "It wasn't

97

as bad as I expected."

She remained silent until they got into a cab.

"Do you want to go for a meal?" he asked her.

"The only thing I want to eat is you," she replied.

Piers gave the driver his home address.

Anne asked: "What did you think of the Rangoon Philharmonic?"

"I can't say I liked the music," he said. "I did think some of the things the guitarist did were interesting. You couldn't call them a pop group. And they weren't sufficiently dependent upon blues intervals to be called jazz. Yet they certainly don't count as classical musicians."

They were both quiet then, until they got home. As soon as they got inside the door Anne said: "Let's go to bed now."

Piers simply nodded. He went into the kitchen and took a bottle of champagne from the concrete pantry floor. He put it in a silver bucket with ice and water. Then he took the box of cigarettes and the table-lighter from the drawing-room, and took everything into the bedroom.

Anne sat on the bed, with her knees tucked under her, wearing a long white robe with innumerable hook-and-eye fasteners down its front. Piers placed the wine, cigarettes and lighter beside the bed and undressed quickly. He put on a silk dressing-gown.

He sat facing her on the bed, with his legs crossed, and began to undo her robe. His excitement grew fast as he exposed her breasts. He cupped them in his hands, caressed them, then bent his head to kiss them. She held his head and stroked his hair. "I like this," she said throatily.

She lay back on the bed, pulling him with her. Her breasts flattened into a new shape. She squeezed them with her own hands, pushing them together and upwards as if offering them to him. Her pelvis moved slowly against his stomach.

Piers shifted in the bed. He ran his lips over her belly, then up the inside of her thigh. She began to groan rhythmically and arch herself against him.

She lifted her legs and rested her heels on his shoulder blades, holding his head with her hands. She took control now, and then suddenly she was there, with a long deep satisfied animal grunt.

He crawled back up the bed until his head was on the pillow beside hers. She smiled into his eyes. "Thank you, darling," she said. Then she rolled him on to his back, knelt between his knees.

Piers felt himself losing control. "Don't," he said. "I can't last."

She lifted her head reluctantly.

"Inside—please," he whispered.

She straddled his hips, kneeling upright, and guided him. He sat up and crossed his legs, so that she was perched in his lap. They began to move slowly, awkwardly at first, until they discovered the best way. Piers tensed his stomach muscles as she pressed into him. She arched her back, proffering her breasts. The brown nipples seemed larger, and the skin of her breasts was stretched tight, as if they were swollen.

The position seemed to dull Piers' passion, making his imminent orgasm recede. But it had the opposite effect on Anne. She breathed in great hungry gulps, crushing his body to her as if to fuse the two together. She moved his lips from one breast to the other and back again, her fingers digging painfully into his scalp. Finally her near-hysteria worked on Piers, and he began to groan helplessly. "Anne," he moaned. "Anne, I can't help it . . ." Suddenly she was screaming and hurling her body against him in ecstasy. He toppled slowly backwards as he poured himself into her in a series of uncontrollable jerks.

They lay in an exhausted tangle of limbs, too breathless to speak, for several minutes. Anne rolled off him then, and lay with an arm and a leg thrown across his body and her face pressed into his neck.

Piers whispered: "You're incredible."

She touched his lips with her fingertips. "You too," she said.

A minute later he said: "Anne?"

"Mmmm?"

"Do you think we're in l-l-love?"

There was a sudden silence as she stopped breathing. Piers felt a warm tear fall on his chest and realised she was crying. The untouched champagne bottle, in its bucket beside the bed, settled noisily in the melting ice.

# Six

Roper completed the Ximenes crossword in the colour supplement and put the magazine down on the drawing-room carpet. He and Anne had woken up late. For breakfast they had drunk the champagne which had lain untouched all night. It had been slightly warm, but they had enjoyed it. Then she had telephoned a taxi to take her to her flat in Chelsea. Piers had wanted her to stay all day Sunday, but she had insisted on going home, and pointed out that they could hardly return to the Midlands together—everyone would guess they had spent the weekend together, and that would hardly do. After she had left Piers had cast around for some occupation to clear his head of the tumbling, split-screen erotic images which were his hangover from two nights with her. The crossword had worked.

He sighed, got up from the chair, and went into his bedroom. Its windows faced west, and so it was shadowed and cool at this time of day. During the afternoon it would get hot.

He sat down at an antique desk fitted into an alcove. He flicked on the spotlight on one side, and pulled a portable electric typewriter towards him. It was time he began to justify his £100,000 a year.

He slipped a sheet of foolscap paper into the roller and began to write his first report to Palmer. He typed quickly and accurately, using all ten fingers, erasing occasional errors with a small white rectangle of Tipp-Ex.

He gave full details of all the new cars Holmes planned to release during the next twelve months. Most of them were modifications of the existing models, but Piers dealt extensively with the new lorries which were Anthony Loughton's pride and joy. He included accurate specifications, prices, marketing strategy, and occasionally picked up a pencil and made a small, rough sketch of some engineering innovation. Later, when he was fully organised, his reports would include blueprints and photocopies of essential documents.

When he had finished there was a stack of foolscap sheets beside the typewriter and a small mountain of cigarette ends in the ashtray.

He opened a drawer in the desk and took out a black leather document case. From it he drew a copy of the Holmes house magazine.

On an inside page was a report headed: "Pools group hit the jackpot." It told how a syndicate of nineteen Holmes employees had won £20,000 on the football pools. There was a large picture of the men, smiling and giving the thumbs-up sign. Briggs, the foundry supervisor who ran the syndicate, was in the centre holding a cheque. Roper looked at the list of names under the caption.

There were shop-floor workers from all over the factory: machine hands, cleaners, fitters, toolmakers, clerical staff. Two names caught Piers' eye: one was a security guard and the other a handyman in the maintenance department. Both might have access to confidential information: the security man on his patrols, and the handyman by virtue of the fact that he would be called upon to repair chairs, air-conditioners and light fittings in the design studios.

Piers tore the page out of the magazine and underlined their names, plus that of Briggs. On the top of the glossy sheet of paper he wrote: "Twenty-four hour surveillance for fourteen days, please."

Then he put the page with his report in an envelope and went out to phone Palmer from a call-box.

"Mr. Leon of Creative Advertising is on the line, sir," said

Roper's secretary. Piers looked at his watch.

"Ask him to ring me in ten minutes' time," he replied. He put the phone down and took a small circular object, about the size of a 10p piece but thicker, from his waistcoat pocket. He would kill two birds with one stone, he decided.

He walked out to his secretary's office. "I'll be with Mr. Dean when Leon comes on again," he said.

He went up in the lift and along the corridor to Dean's room. "Mr. Dean alone?" he said to the Managing Director's secretary.

"Yes, Mr. Roper."

Piers tapped on the door and walked in. Dean looked up from his desk.

"Busy, Larry?" said Roper.

"Sit down, Piers."

"I'm thinking of firing our advertising agency," Roper began.

"You're the boss in that department," Dean replied. Suddenly he winced with pain. He threw a key on his intercom and told his secretary: "Glass of water, Andrea."

"Ulcer?" Piers inquired.

"Headaches." Dean took a bottle of pills from a drawer and palmed three. His secretary came in with a glass and a bottle of mineral water on a tray.

Piers continued: "I just wanted to check with you in case there was a particular reason you wanted to keep them."

Dean put all three pills in his mouth and swallowed them with a gulp of water. "No particular reason," he said.

His phone rang. He picked it up, listened for a moment, and said: "It's for you, Piers. Leon from the ad agency. Take it here—I have to go to the gents', anyway."

Roper took the phone from him and watched him leave. "Hello," he said.

"Piers, it's Tony Leon."

"Good. Can you get here in the next few days?"

"Will the middle of next week do?"

"Yes."

"Wednesday, then."

"Come down in time for lunch."

"Will do, Piers."

"Bye." Roper jiggled the rest and got Dean's secretary. "Give me an outside line, please," he asked her.

When the dialling tone purred he rang the Speaking Clock. "—and forty seconds," said the mechanical voice. Piers swiftly unscrewed the mouthpiece of the handset. He took the circular object from his waistcoat pocket and slid it inside the receiver, fixing it with a tiny piece of Elastoplast. Then he assembled the handset again and replaced it on the phone. Dean walked in.

"So you're going to fire Leon," he said.

"I think so. It's never a bad thing to switch agencies after a couple of years. They get stale, you know. A new one is always so eager to keep the account they flog themselves to death to please you. And this is quite a good time. The only major thing that's going is the Capricorn booster campaign."

"Does Leon know anything that could be useful to anyone else?" Dean asked.

"No. He knows we're launching a new lorry, but he doesn't know the details yet. In fact, he probably thinks that's what we want to see him about."

"Okay, Piers."

Roper got up and went out. Back in his office, he unlocked a desk drawer and took out what looked like a packet of Senior Service. He slid the packet open to reveal a small radio receiver. He put it to his ear, adjusted a volume control on the side, and heard Dean say: "—me know the latest costing on the body plant extension—" Piers put the machine away. The Managing Director's office was successfully bugged.

It was four o'clock. Roper decided to leave early. As he went down in the lift, he ran over the pros and cons of what he had just done. He ought to be able to get all the information he needed by perfectly above-board means—after all, he was a senior executive of the company. But the bug was a kind of insurance. There might be internal plotting in the firm which he needed to know about in order to maintain his position. And, most importantly, if anyone suspected Piers of leaking information, the bug would enable him to find out about it.

He drove into the centre of the town and left the car in the underground car park of his hotel.

His weeknight evenings were becoming more and more of a pain. He and Anne had agreed it would be indiscreet to see each other except in London. So he spent most evenings in his room, drinking rather too much. He could not remember what he had done with himself before he met her.

He walked along the main shopping street of the town now, looking for the local hi-fi shop. Perhaps some music would help to pass the long summer evenings. He found the shop and went in.

An assistant in a badly fitting suit asked whether he could help. The man had long hair and acne.

"I want a fairly cheap stereo," Piers said. "It must have headphones."

"The headphones usually come separately, but most of the good outfits have a socket for them," the man said. "How much do you want to spend?"

"About £150," Piers replied.

The assistant showed him three seats. All sounded perfectly good through the headphones, and Piers chose the best-looking one. He signed a cheque and asked to have the hi-fi delivered to his hotel room.

When he left the shop the pavements were becoming crowded with the first wave of homegoing office workers. He walked along until he came to a pop record shop. In fact it was half a shop: the original premises had been divided down the middle, and the other half was now a tobacconists.

Inside were racks of record sleeves in polythene dust covers all along one wall. Acoustic booths filled the opposite wall, leaving a narrow gangway down the shop to the counter at the far end where a young girl stood chewing gum and looking bored. Above the display racks were arty blown-up photographs of what Piers presumed were musicians. The acoustic booths, where a couple of people were listening to records, were inadequately soundproofed, and a cacophony of discordant music emerged.

Piers tried to remember the name of the group Anne had taken him to see. All that would come into his head was the name Rangoon Philharmonic. He went over to a rack of records and began thumbing them as he tried to think. Finally the name came.

He went up to the counter and said: "Have you any records of the Mahavishnu Orchestra?"

"What label are they on?" the girl replied.

"I've no idea."

"Well I can't look them up if I don't know the label."

A man came out of a door behind the counter. The girl turned to him and said: "Have we got the . . ."

Piers supplied: "Mahavishnu Orchestra."

"Of course," the man said. He smiled at Piers. "Which did you want?"

"I'll take them all."

"There are only two," the man said. He bent to a shelf and picked out two records.

"Thank you," Piers said, and got out his wallet.

"It's nice to serve someone with good taste," the man said unctuously as he put the discs into a bag. "We get more demand for Gary Glitter here."

"Who?" said Piers.

The man laughed, as if Piers had been joking.

When he got back to the hotel there was a telephone message from London, from an art dealer Roper patronised.

When he had washed he picked up the phone and asked for the number on the message.

"Ah, Mr. Beaumont," he said when he got through.

"Thank you for returning my call, Mr. Roper. I have a chance of a picture I think you will be interested in. It's a small Andre Derain still life of about 1921. Most attractive."

"What is it called?" Piers asked.

"Still Life Sunlit," the dealer replied.

"I think I know it," Piers replied. "A very olive-greenish thing."

"That's it. It has been exhibited a couple of times, but it was in private ownership. I think I can get it for four figures."

"Fine," Piers said. "I did know who owned it, but I can't remember off-hand."

"I'm afraid I don't know. It's in the hands of another dealer. Shall I acquire it for you?"

"Please," Piers said.

"Splendid."

"And thank you for calling."

"Goodbye."

Piers hung up, put on his jacket, and went down to the hotel cocktail bar to celebrate.

"I hear you're about to fire us," said Tony Leon.

Roper stared at the man. He wore a beautiful oatmeal suit with a pale lemon shirt, and his dark brown beard was neatly trimmed. He was almost as tall as Piers, but stockier, and he had deceptively lazy brown eyes.

"How did you hear that?" Roper asked.

Leon tapped the side of his nose by way of reply. I shouldn't be surprised, Piers thought. The only way to keep a secret in this business is to tell absolutely no one.

Piers said: "And now you're going to tell me why I shouldn't."

"You got it."

Piers sat back in his chair. "You have the floor," he said.

"A few weeks back we hired a new man," Leon said. "He came from Medium." He paused for effect. Piers looked blank.

"They have the English Motors account," the advertising man explained. Piers' interest quickened.

"Before he came to us he was working on a campaign for a new lorry," Leon continued. "I thought you might be interested in it." He picked up his briefcase and took out a sheaf of drawings.

Piers held out his hand. Leon grinned. "Are we hired again?" he said.

"You're hired." Piers took the drawings. He looked through them with an increasing sense of shock. They were prototype adverts for a range of lorries practically identical with the ones Holmes were planning.

Leon said: "Don't worry—those aren't stolen property. The boy did them again from memory for me."

"You've no way of knowing how important these are," Piers said. The implications of the sketches were turning cartwheels in his brain. "Listen, Tony. I don't want you to mention this to anyone else here for a while."

"Whatever you say."

"Or, indeed, anyone else anywhere."

"Of course."

"And I want to postpone discussion of the campaign for our lorry for a while. When is the launch date for these ads of English's?"

"A month or so. They hadn't finalised when our boy left."

"My God. That soon."

"Shall I leave you to study them?"

"Please, Tony. I'm sorry to send you back to town so quickly."

"Don't worry. I bought a day return." Leon smiled quickly. "I'll be seeing you." As he left, Piers forgot to say goodbye.

He took from his locked drawer Palmer's report to him on

the surveillance of Briggs and his cronies. He put the report on top of the sketches. The two just did not hang together.

The sketches showed that English Motors were bringing out a range of lorries so similar to Holmes's that it could not be coincidence. The ads mentioned design innovations, including the revolutionary suspension, which had to be stolen. It betrayed a very high level of espionage within Holmes.

Of course, Piers had passed full details of the Holmes lorries to Palmer, who would have forwarded them to English. But that had only been a few weeks ago. The other source must have been working for English for over a year.

Clearly, Lennon's men had penetrated Holmes at the very top. That was where the surveillance of Briggs came in.

Palmer's agents had seen Briggs pass money to a handful of Holmes employees. He had also received a few documents, usually wrapped up in pools coupons. One agent had got hold of one of the documents and it was enclosed with the report. It was a very unimportant job card for a toolmaking task in the research department. The information passed, and the money which changed hands in Briggs' espionage outfit was all very low-level. The man had no contacts in the upper echelons of the firm, and none in really crucial places like the test beds.

The possibility of a third espionage outfit supplying information about Holmes to English seemed far fetched. It was almost certainly Lennon's men. But they certainly weren't getting their information through Briggs' network.

Piers was stumped.

He stopped the Bentley on the grass verge of the narrow country road. Beside the verge was a high hedge broken by a little gate.

"Now perhaps you'll tell me what this is all about," said Anne. They had broken their rule about not meeting during the week. Piers had said only that he wanted to show her something. They had driven thirty miles out of the town, along a route Piers obviously knew.

"Let's get out and look at it," he said now. He opened her door and led her across the grass to the gate. When he tried to open it, it fell over. They stepped across it.

"There," said Piers, and pointed.

"I see," Anne said with a smile.

They were standing in front of a low-roofed cottage. In fact it was two semi-detached cottages with a common front garden and path. They had small leaded windows and a slate roof with a central chimney.

Piers and Anne walked up to the front. "I came out here with the estate agent last night," he said. He took a key from his pocket and opened the door on the left-hand side of the common porch.

The kitchen was in front of them, with an old-fashioned boiler on one side. On the left was a step up to the living-room. A door off the living-room led to a bedroom.

"The two cottages are mirror-images of one another," Piers explained. "I could knock the two kitchens into one, and demolish the wall between the living-room and the bedroom in here to make a big drawing-room. The place has been empty a while, but it's dry."

"It's lovely," Anne said. "At least, it will be, after it's been worked on. You're going to buy it, then?"

"If you like it." He saw her raised eyebrows, and added: "I'd like to hope you might spend some time here when I've moved in."

She took his hand. "Of course I will," she smiled.

"I've bought our first picture for the place," he said. He took a crumpled old gallery catalogue from his inside pocket and proffered it.

She looked at it. "Oh!" she exclaimed. "Did you buy it from Sir Trevor?"

"What?" Piers said incredulously.

Piers went into Holmes' Public Relations Department first thing the following morning. It was a big, open-plan office. On a table by the door were several copies of each of the morning papers. A typist looked up from her work and said: "Yes sir?"

"It's all right, Pat," said a young man behind her. He got up and came around his desk. Roper recognised him as James Hudson, the former Birmingham Post reporter who was now Holmes' Press Officer.

"Oh, Hello, Hudson," said Piers. The young man looked pleased that Piers remembered his name. "I'd like to look at the press cuttings."

"Certainly. Come with me." Hudson led him into a small ante-room. Huge hardbacked scrapbooks were stored on shelves around the walls. The young man waved a hand at the books. "We have a number of sections: one for each main model of car, one for the company generally, one for industrial trouble, and one for the firm's personnel. Within the sections the cuttings are ordered chronologically."

"Which is the personnel section?"

"Here," Hudson said. There was a pile of the books stacked six feet high. Piers sighed at the task which confronted him.

"How far back do we go?" he asked.

"About fifty years, in this room. There are older records—"

"That's fine," Piers interrupted. "All right, Hudson, thanks for your help."

The man took the hint. "I'll be just outside if there's anything else, sir," he said, and backed out of the door.

Piers pulled a book marked "1963–68" out of the stack. The article he was looking for was somewhere in that period, he felt sure.

Twenty minutes later he had found it. It was a piece from a magazine, one of a series of articles on art collectors. This one was about Sir Trevor Hollowood. There was a small colour photograph of the Derain which Piers had just bought.

He must have read the article when it appeared, and noticed the painting then. The fact that it belonged to Sir Trevor had lodged in his subconscious. Anne had seen the painting at Sir Trevor's house, and remembered it as soon as Piers showed her the catalogue. Her recollection that it had belonged to Sir Trevor had jogged Piers' memory and reminded him of the article.

Piers wondered why Sir Trevor should sell it. He had a hunch about the answer.

He read through the article, making a note of all the paintings mentioned as belonging to Sir Trevor. It was a fairly impressive collection, mainly late nineteenth-century modern art, with a sprinkling of slightly later work like the Derain, of the period Roper favoured.

He folded his sheet of notes, put it in his pocket, and replaced the cuttings book. As he walked back through the PR office he said to Hudson: "Very efficient."

"Thank you," the young man said with a smile.

In his own office he telephoned his art dealer in London.

"I want to ask you a favour, Mr. Beaumont," he began.

"Please do."

"I wonder if you could put one of your people on to a little research job for me. I have a list of twenty-two paintings here, and I'm wondering how many of them have come on the market recently."

"I may be able to tell you from memory. Run down the list."

Piers read out the names of the paintings mentioned in the article. When he had finished Beaumont said: "Well, that's easy. Almost all of them have been disposed of during the past year or so. I know because the dealer who sold them is a contact of mine."

"The same chap who put the Derain your way?"

"Indeed. Of course, the others were not quite in your line—"

"No, no, that's all right. Tell me, how long ago was the first of them sold?"

"Let me see." There was a moment's pause. "That would be the Pissarro, which went last May, so twelve months ago."

"Mr. Beaumont, your knowledge is encyclopaedic. Thank you very much."

"Anything to oblige, Mr. Roper. Are you pleased with the Derain, by the way?"

"Delighted. I'm buying a new house to hang it in."

Beaumont laughed politely. "Splendid," he said.

"Goodbye, Mr. Beaumont." Piers hung up.

He sat back and lit a cigarette. He had brought the straight-backed leather arm-chair from his flat to replace the swivelling instrument of torture which had been in the office originally. He sat comfortably in it now, with his elbows on the arms and his hands clasped across his chest, a cigarette burning in his long fingers. He tried to calculate the value of the paintings Sir Trevor Hollowood had sold in the past year.

Hollowood was reputed to be a rich man. He owned a lot of Holmes stock, and he was the major shareholder in an investment company. There was also a family firm, Hollowood Mechanical, and his wife had independent wealth. He spent a few weeks every year at his house in Jamaica, and had a yacht moored in the Mediterranean somewhere.

Piers wondered why he had suddenly needed half a million pounds.


Roper spread the mock-up advertisements over the desk and floor of Anthony Loughton's office. "Our agency came across these," he told Loughton. "They hired a man from English's agency, who brought the information with him."

Loughton stared at the drawings. "Oh, my God," he said softly.

A corner of one sheet rolled itself up defiantly. Piers took off his watch and placed it on the corner as a paperweight.

"This is our new lorry," Loughton said.

"And they're six months ahead of us," Piers added.

"The design—the new suspension—the concept of the range—everything," Loughton went on. "How did you get hold of these?"

"I told you. Our agency—"

"Yes, I see. Bloody hell, that tears it."

"What do you think is the explanation?"

"Espionage," Loughton said immediately. Piers raised his eyebrows. "Of course it is," Loughton went on. "They've been spying on us—God knows how they did it. They've had our blueprints, research projects, test results, the lot. They must have, to do this and come out ahead of us. When did you say their launch date was?"

"I didn't. But it's only a matter of weeks."

"The bastards," Loughton said bitterly. "What the hell are we going to tell Larry?"

"The whole truth, I imagine."

"It'll kill him. You're right, of course."

"Where does this leave Holmes as a whole, Tony?"

Loughton looked sharply at Piers. "Up against the bloody wall. You know that."

"What I meant was, where does the company go next?"

"I know the answer to that," Loughton replied. "America."

Piers looked thoughtful.

"Well, we might as well go straight to Larry Dean," Loughton said. He took his jacket from the back of the chair behind his desk and shrugged into it. "After you," he said, holding the door open.

In the corridor Piers stopped. "I left my watch," he said. "Go on ahead while I go back for it."

In the ante-room to Loughton's office he took a folded sheet of paper from his pocket and gave it to the secretary. "Would you take this down to my office?" he asked her. He watched her leave and then went into Loughton's office.

He lifted the phone and unscrewed the mouthpiece. Inside he fixed an electronic listening device identical to the one he had put in Dean's phone. He quickly fitted the phone together again. There had been no one in the secretary's office to see the light come on on her telephone. He slipped his watch on his wrist and went out.

Inkleman, the Production Executive, arrived at Dean's office at the same time as Roper. Lord Shipley was already there with Dean and Loughton. Hollowood, Jones of Design and Giddins of Personnel came in a minute later.

They saw the grim expression on Loughton's face, and sensed the simmering anger in Dean. They waited nervously, curiously, to be told the reason for the MD's peremptory summons.

When they were seated Dean said: "You'd better tell it, Piers."

Roper explained quickly what he had discovered about the new English lorry. As he was speaking he noticed Dean take the bottle of tablets from his desk drawer and swallow some without water.

When Piers finished speaking there was a shocked silence. Eventually Inkleman spoke.

"I can't help thinking that this is a consequence of a decision we took a couple of years ago," he said. "We made up our minds not to accept a bid from America which would have given us a big injection of capital."

"And a pair of handcuffs," Dean said.

"Nevertheless, we decided to fight the American-backed English Motors with our own resources. This is the result," Inkleman persisted.

"We don't need recriminations," Dean said irritably. "I want ideas, not I-told-you-so's."

Inkleman's tone became bitter. "It needs to be said that the financial decisions this company has made over the past couple of years have been bad ones. Take Selectronics if you want another example."

The atmosphere in the room was becoming tense very quickly, Piers noted. The executives saw their reputations threatened and their careers blighted. They were men who worked incredibly hard, and dedicated their lives to their profession. When they sensed ruin over the horizon, they looked for someone to blame. Now old quarrels were being dragged out as alibis. He made a mental note to look up Selectronics.

Loughton stood up. "Let me think aloud for a minute, and try to put this thing into perspective," he said. He walked around his chair and sat on the edge of a table up against the wall.

"The activity of this company runs in waves. We introduce a new model. Its sales peak anything from six months to two years after the launch, then start to stagnate. But by the time this begins, we reckon to have paid off the capital costs of a new model.

"This is the time when we make big profits from the vehicle. It is also the time we start spending those profits on new investment for the next model. So that by the time the old model stops making money, we've got a new one to take its place."

Dean interrupted: "All this is—"

But Jones, in turn, interrupted Dean. "For Christ's sake, Larry," he said.

"Just let me finish this thought," Loughton went on. "This year we have two main new models: the Capricorn and the lorry range. According to the cyclic model of the company's activity which I've been talking about, next year should be a year of lower investment and rising profits. We anticipate rising sales of the two new models, without any major capital outlay to cut into the profits. But English Motors have changed all that.

"Because of *their* new lorry, and the Diamond, the sales of

116

our models will be anything from ten to fifty per cent below forecast.

"And the result of *that* is twofold. One: we need our next batch of new models much sooner, in order to retain our grip on the market. Two: we haven't got the capital to put into a new model, because our profits slump.

"It's obvious where this line of thinking ends. We have to look outside the company for a big fat loan."

Now Piers realised that the old quarrel which had been revived at the start of the discussion was more relevant than he had imagined. Holmes had to look for capital, and the executives were already lining up into factions: those who favoured an American takeover, and those who did not. He remembered the way the split ran: Dean, Shipley, Hollowood and himself versus Loughton, Inkleman, Jones and Giddins. He wondered whether there would be any defections.

He decided to effect a polarisation. "At the risk of stating the obvious, I might say that the possibilities in that direction are of two kinds: British and American."

Dean looked at Hollowood. "What's the money market like, Trevor?" he said.

That was a nice move, Piers thought. It was the cue for Sir Trevor to come down in favour of going to the City rather than Wall Street for the money. It gave the anti-American faction the opportunity to fire the first shot.

But Sir Trevor surprised him. The Financial Director said: "I think we would have to get the whole lump from one source. Without looking into the problem in detail, my guess is that a merger of some kind is the only answer."

Piers saw the shock register on Dean's face.

"I can't understand that," Piers said. He knew that a merger could only mean the Americans. "Couldn't we combine a set of money-raising operations: some permutation of share issue, overdraft, rearrangement of our cash flow, and straight commercial loans?"

"The short answer to that is No," Hollowood said. "It's because of the way we have financed the Capricorn and the new lorry. It would take a while to explain it all, but the bare fact is we've exhausted our borrowing capacity in short and middle-term money."

Dean's face had reddened. "I am ashamed to have to say that this comes as a surprise to me," he said.

"I haven't kept these things secret, Larry," Sir Trevor said mildly.

No, but you've kept the implications to yourself, thought Piers. It was an astonishing situation. At a time of crisis, the company suddenly discovers that its liquidity is overstretched.

Piers said: "There is one possibility that you haven't ruled out, Sir Trevor. The Government."

Dean said: "My God." The magnitude of the disaster seemed to have just penetrated the MD's bluster.

Lord Shipley spoke for the first time. "It seems that, for now, what we must do is look more closely at the capital prospects. I suggest Sir Trevor prepares a report on the possibilities, both British and American."

Like a good chairman he had summed up the result of the discussion in a nutshell. Dean nodded in agreement, and Sir Trevor got up. There was an awkward silence, then the other executives began to leave.

Roper left with Loughton. As they walked towards the lift, Piers said quietly: "Why do you think Sir Trevor has sold his art collection?"

Loughton looked startled. "I haven't the faintest idea," he said.

# Seven

Piers lay in bed on Saturday morning, waiting for Anne to wake up, and thought about Sir Trevor Hollowood.

He had looked up the minutes of executive board meetings for the first half of last year, and discovered the story of Selectronics Ltd. It was a medium-sized company which supplied a lot of parts for Holmes' cars. Holmes had contemplated taking the firm over. But despite apparently favourable financial reports, the board had decided not to. The minutes referred to "an extended discussion", which was code for an almighty row.

Piers had returned to London a day early and spent a morning in Companies House. He had discovered that, while Holmes was considering whether to take Selectronics over, there had been a lot of trading in the electronics firm's shares. Eighteen months ago, an investment company had become a major shareholder in Selectronics. The investment company was owned by a holding company: and the biggest shareholder in the holding company was Sir Trevor Hollowood.

The picture was now clear. Against all the rules of financial ethics, Sir Trevor had used his inside information about Holmes to buy Selectronic shares—anticipating selling them at a fat profit when Holmes made its takeover bid. But the executives of Holmes had changed their minds—no wonder there had been a row—and Hollowood had got his fingers badly burned.

That explained why the man was in such severe financial trouble that he had to sell his art collection. And it led to a speculative equation: was the Holmes director who was badly short of cash the same as the highly-placed executive who was selling secrets to the opposition?

Piers would have been satisfied to jump to that conclusion, had it not been for Hollowood's behaviour in Dean's office during the crisis meeting.

Two things had been revealed then. The first was that Hollowood had changed sides in the conflict over whether to merge with an American company. The second was that he seemed to have manipulated the Holmes finances so that they now had little alternative but to merge. Neither of these was explained by his being short of cash.

Piers felt as if there was one piece of the jigsaw missing, and when he found it he would be able to understand the picture.

Anne stirred, and yawned without opening her eyes. Piers got out of bed and went to the kitchen to put on coffee. He did not bother to put on a dressing-gown. Before he had met Anne, he would have put one on even if he had been alone in the flat. The list of habits he had dropped in the last couple of months must be very long, he thought as he waited for the coffee to brew.

He went to the second bedroom and pulled a framed painting away from the wall to reveal a small safe. He spun the dial to the combination, opened the door, and took out a box about the size of a paperback. It was wrapped in purple paper and tied with a ribbon.

He went back to the kitchen and took a pen and a small white card from a drawer. He stood looking at the bubbling coffee pot trying to think what to write on the card. He considered "I love you" and rejected it immediately. He did not know what the phrase really meant; besides, the one time he had used the word "love" it had had an effect which he still did not understand. In the end he wrote "I thank you" and slipped the card under the ribbon. He was not very happy with the message. It was the kind of thing a London bus conductor said when he took your fare. Still, it was what he wanted to say to Anne with this gift.

The coffee was ready. He poured two cups, taking care not to splash the hot liquid on his bare skin. Then he put cups and parcel on a tray and carried them into the bedroom.

She was awake. She had thrown the bed-clothes back, and lay stretched out on her back. Her hands were clasped above her head, and the sparse hair of her underarms echoed the shadow between her legs. Piers suddenly felt the odd desire to bury his face in her armpit; and marvelled again at the lust she could arouse in him.

"It's hot," she said.

Piers placed the tray beside her. He went over to the window and opened it wide. The fresh air which blew in gently was warm. The sun was high, and in an hour or so it would come around and shine in through the window. Piers looked at the narrow fire-escape verandah just below the window. Low wrought-iron railings ran along the edge of it. A man on a ladder was repainting the railings at the far end, covering the flaking old paintwork with swift, expert strokes. Down in the street nothing moved. Belgravia was dead on Saturday mornings.

Piers turned back into the room. "Why don't you shave your underarms?" he asked Anne.

"Because I hate to look like a tart in a cheap nudie magazine," she replied. "Why, do you object to hairy underarms?"

"No. I just thought all women shaved them." He sat on the edge of the bed and handed her a cup of coffee. She sat upright and took it.

"This is for you," he said, handing her the gift. Her eyes, already big and liquid, widened impossibly.

"It's not even my birthday," she said. She read the card. The look she gave him was unreadable.

"Open it," he said.

She untied the ribbon and removed the wrapping, revealing a velvet box. She lifted the lid.

Inside was the gold watch they had seen priced at £367.50

in the window of the Regent Street jewellers.

"Oh, Piers, it's that watch," she said.

"That was our first weekend together—do you remember?"

She touched his hand. "Of course I remember," she said thickly. Inexplicably, her eyes filled with tears. He leaned forward to kiss her.

As their lips met, a small part of his mind heard a small click. It was so faint as to be almost inaudible. It could have been a spoon shifting in a saucer, or the mattress yielding to new pressures. Piers reacted instinctively.

He jerked away from Anne like a twanged bowstring, every taut muscle moving in a co-ordinated swing. His training came back to him as if Army Intelligence had been yesterday instead of twenty years ago: he dropped on all fours to get out of the line of fire and crossed the floor to the open window in a blurred forward roll. As he came off the floor and reached for the window-sill a shadow moved on the verandah outside. Piers vaulted the sill and landed with his back to the railings.

He struck out at the shadow, landing four piston punches in a second. Then he grabbed the man's clothing and pushed him backwards through the window into the bedroom. He jumped through afterwards, landing with his knee in the man's belly.

Anne screamed.

Piers looked at the fellow. It was the painter he had seen working on the railings. A small camera was attached to his wrist. That explained the click which Piers' instinct had taken for the safety catch of a revolver: in fact it had been the shutter opening.

The man was still now, giving Piers a chance to think. Somebody wanted pictures of Piers Roper and Anne Mainwaring in bed together.

The immediate necessity was to get the camera away from the man. It was attached to his wrist by a leather strap. Piers said to Anne: "Scissors, quickly."

"Piers, who is he?" she said in a strained, frightened voice.

"Questions later, fool!" he shouted. "Get me the scissors."

She got out of bed, rummaged in her bag, and handed him a pair of nail scissors. He cut the leather strap on the camera. It was a tiny Japanese precision model, very expensive. He threw it on the bed.

"Now let's take a good look at you," he said to the painter. The man had lank black hair, cut short at the sides and back, with a long lock hanging over one eye. His face was shadowed with a day's growth of dark beard, and his eyes were brown under heavy brows. The mouth was wide and thin lipped.

Piers had never seen him before.

The man lay on the floor with Piers kneeling on his belly. "Who are you?" Piers said.

The man did not reply. Piers got to his feet, picked the man up, and slammed him against the wall. He punched his face twice, with hammer-like blows that rocked the man's head against the wall with two sickening thuds. Blood poured from his nose and mouth. He swung a kick, but Piers moved easily aside, caught the foot, and lifted. The painter fell to the floor. Piers stamped on the man's genitals with a heel. There was a grunt of pain—the first sound the man had made.

Piers noticed his gloves. Painters did not wear gloves.

"He's a professional," he muttered. To the man he said: "Who hired you?"

The man lay on the floor, moaning softly.

Piers picked up the nail scissors from the carpet. He dug the points into the man's temple and slashed down his cheek to his mouth. He screamed in agony.

"Piers, stop it!" Anne sobbed.

Roper had forgotten she was there. He looked up in surprise. The painter saw his chance. With a quick movement of his feet, he kicked Piers' legs from under him. Piers hit the floor.

The painter was on his feet in a split second. Piers swung one arm blindly, and the man staggered against the wall beside

123

the open window. Piers came off the floor swinging a punch. It caught the man in the solar plexus. He pulled his arm back for a second blow. Anne yelled again, and caught his arm. The painter aimed a kick at Piers' groin. The heavy shoe landed painfully. The painter leapt out of the window.

Piers realised that, naked, he could not chase the man. He clutched his genitals and snapped at Anne: "You damn fool, I've lost him now."

Tears were streaming down her face. "But Piers, you would have killed him."

"Why the hell not," he muttered. He limped over to the bed and sat down.

Anne's eyes were staring, as if she were seeing again the scene which had passed. "Oh!" she said, and shivered. Almost to herself, she whispered: "You were like an animal. An animal."

Piers got up and put on his pants to ease the ache in his testicles. He picked up the camera, opened the back, and unrolled the film, making sure every square inch of light-sensitive cellulose was exposed. Then he threw the lot in the paper-bin beside his desk.

The ache eased, and he got up. He walked up and down the room, turning over the implications of what had happened in his mind. There were two main possibilities: it could be a straightforward blackmail attempt by someone who knew Piers was rich and had a mistress. But in these days of permissiveness, the fact that a bachelor and a divorcee were spending their nights together was hardly blackmail material.

Unless the bachelor was a top executive and the divorcee was a company employee. The pictures the painter had been taking could have done Piers a lot of damage within Holmes. So the blackmailer—who was almost certainly not the painter himself, but someone who had employed the painter—knew something about the Holmes Motor Corporation. Which led to the second possibility: that the blackmailer did not want money, but just needed a lever to make Piers do his will in the executive boardroom.

And he needed it badly, to resort to such cloak-and-dagger tactics. Nothing Piers could do in the company would justify the risk. Unless . . .

Of course. Piers *did* have enormous power over Sir Trevor Hollowood, now that he knew the director's guilty secret. The blackmailer could be Sir Trevor, looking for a weapon with which to defend himself against Piers.

It was a good possibility, and the best he could do with mere speculation. He turned to Anne. She was sitting on the bed, staring at him with her unforgettable big eyes. She realised she had his attention at last.

She said: "I just had no idea you could be so . . . brutal." She shuddered. Piers nodded. It occurred to him that when his reflexes had taken him down, out of the line of fire of the imagined rifle, he had exposed Anne to a bullet. It was that brutalism which shocked him: but she was talking about the beating he had given the painter.

He opened his mouth to say something conciliatory.

Anne said: "Don't speak, Piers."

He frowned in puzzlement.

She lay back on the bed and opened her legs in a flagrantly carnal gesture. "Just come and fuck with me—quickly."

Piers took the lift from the underground car park to the ground floor of the hotel. He went into the cocktail bar and took his usual corner seat. The waiter nodded at the quiet, handsome man who had become so familiar over the weeks. Without waiting to be asked, he poured a double whisky into a glass and added an equal quantity of water, then carried it to the man's table.

Piers put a cigarette in his mouth. The waiter's lighter was out in a flash. Piers dipped the end of the Senior Service in the flame and nodded his thanks. The waiter moved away.

Piers took a long sip of the drink. He enjoyed it—it was the first of the day. He had disciplined himself not to drink before five, after he had realised he had got into the habit of putting away seven or eight whiskies at lunchtime. Even now, in the empty cocktail bar, he felt a little decadent as the alcohol seeped into his bloodstream and soothed his addiction.

It was Wednesday, the worst evening of the week: the day most distant from his weekends with Anne. He drained his glass and raised his eyebrows at the waiter, who promptly brought the same again. Piers picked up a copy of the local evening newspaper and ran his eye over the front page. He read an agency report about the day's trading in sterling and ignored the rest of the news. Inside, he ploughed carefully through the entertainment guide in case there was something he had missed in the same paper on Monday night. The town's cinemas boasted one British comedy, one sex film, and a French film he had seen in the West End a year ago. There was no classical music and no live theatre. He flicked through the rest of the paper, scanning the boring, sensational headlines, and dropped it on the seat beside him.

The waiter brought a third double Scotch, and Piers realised he had emptied his glass again. He got out another cigarette, and whipped out his own lighter before the waiter could oblige. Afterwards he was disgusted by his own childishness.

A couple in their forties came into the bar. The man was overweight, and carried himself with a cavalier air which sat ill on his clumsy body. Piers observed the way the woman looked at him, and decided the two were having an affair. He looked away.

The clock crept around to six-thirty, and Piers went in to dinner early. As he ate, he pondered the Holmes case. It was clear that smashing the Lennon gang was now his first priority, as any information he passed to Palmer was certain to be old hat to English Motors.

He felt he was losing his grip on the case: no, it was not that

126

—he had never gained a grip on it. Events were not in his control. He was following instead of manipulating the course of the crisis within the company. He felt impotent, and—what was worse—apathetic.

He carved his steak with a serrated-edge stainless steel knife. The outside of the meat was hard-baked, and at its centre it was still deep frozen. The knife crunched on iced blood. Piers summoned the waiter and explained to him, in a quiet but clear voice, what was wrong. The waiter was surly, but a minute later the chef came hurrying out of the kitchen and apologised with Gallic profusion. Piers began to wish he had simply left the meal untouched. When the replacement steak arrived, it was brought by the chef himself, and was perfectly cooked.

Piers refused the sweet, cheeseboard, and coffee, and went up to his room. He rang down for a bottle of Scotch and a jug of water, then went into the bathroom and ran a bath.

He lay in the bath, drinking and smoking, until the water became tepid. When he got out he dressed in black slacks and a red shirt. He had bought a dozen identical to the one Anne had foisted on him.

Finally he put one of the Mahavishnu Orchestra records on the hi-fi he had bought, put on the headphones, and sat in an arm-chair with the whisky and his cigarettes at arm's length.

He tried to analyse the cause of his discontent. It was not the job. That was a good challenge to his professional abilities— something he ought to have enjoyed. It was not the music, although that gave him no pleasure tonight. He heard the record through then took off the headphones and rubbed his itching ears. He poured another drink, and noticed that the bottle was half-empty already. He lit a cigarette and glanced at his watch. The time was passing more quickly now.

The problem, he decided, was Life as a Whole. Whisky had dulled his sensitivity to cliché, which in times of sobriety amounted to a chronic allergy. I have done everything well, he protested to himself. A good mathematician, a good soldier, a good salesman, a good spy. And a good lover, he added as an afterthought. Nowadays he had enough money to satisfy all his material wants, which were expensive for all they would have struck many men as being ascetic.

The level in the bottle sunk lower, and analysis gave way to emotion. And yet, he thought, self-consciously observing the trend, perhaps the answer lies in emotion rather than analysis.

He got up, put on his jacket, and methodically switched off the stereo and the lights. He put his wallet in one pocket, his car keys in another, and his cigarettes and lighter in a third. Then he went out.

He knew he appeared perfectly sober as he walked a straight line through the hotel lobby and down the steps to the street. Five minutes of carefully upright walking took him to the town's meagre red-light district.

In a dim-lit street, a young man with broad shoulders and long blond hair tapped his shoulder and said: "Looking for a lady?"

"Yes," Piers said.

"Twenty-five quid, and she's only eighteen," the pimp said quickly. Piers took out his wallet, thumbed over a wad of notes, and gave the man three tenners. The man saw the wad, snatched the wallet, and turned on his heel. If Piers had been totally sober he would have caught the man's wrist before the hand closed on the wallet. As it was, it took him a split-second to realise what was happening, and he tripped the thief before he had taken his first pace.

The wallet flew across the pavement. Piers swept it up with a quick movement. Before the pimp could get up, Piers kicked his face with a well-aimed brogue. Through the leather, his toe felt the snap of a bone. Piers walked calmly away.

He found the way back to his hotel, and walked down the ramp to the car park. He located the Bentley, got in, and drove precisely along the centre of the narrow roadway to the exit.

On the street, several cars flashed their headlights at him and he realised he had forgotten to switch on his lights.

At exactly 29 mph, he drove out to a suburb and found a street of elderly, tall houses of decayed elegance. He found the number he was looking for. The house was divided into flats, and the front door bore a row of bells with labels beside them. He pressed one.

Through the frosted glass of the door he saw a light come on and a figure descend the stairs. The shape became more clearly defined as it approached the door. Then the frosted glass swung aside to reveal Anne.

Piers said: "I have done everything well, and nothing good. Will you marry me?"

"No," she said, and closed the door.

Roper tapped on the door of Dean's office and walked in. Sir Trevor Hollowood was with the Managing Director, sitting on the corner of the wide desk. The two had a conspiratorial air, and they looked up guiltily at Piers. Dean's expression cleared when he recognised the newcomer.

"Ah, Piers," he said. "Trevor has an interview at the Department of Trade and Industry this afternoon."

"That's a bit sudden," Roper remarked. He knew Hollowood had been trying to arrange to see a senior civil servant informally, to broach the subject of a Government loan to the Holmes Motor Corporation.

"Yes. I imagine they've got a sniff of our troubles. They're always a bit abrupt when they think you're after money," Hollowood said.

"Anyway, I thought we might discuss the best way to go about it," Dean said. "Ever had any contact with the DTI, Piers?"

"No," Roper replied. He realised now why the two of them had looked so secretive when he walked in. This was a faction meeting: the pro-American executives had not been invited.

Except, he reminded himself, that Hollowood was probably a traitor. He wondered whether Dean suspected that.

He sat down and took out his cigarettes. "I imagine this is the broad picture," he began. "Holmes must merge to survive. If we merge with a British company we fall foul of the Monopolies Commission. If we take on American capital, it leaves the British motor industry completely dominated by the USA, which will be politically inconvenient. Therefore we must have Government capital."

"Fine," Dean concurred. "So long as you don't put it quite so bluntly, Trevor. We don't want to seem to be making them an offer they can't refuse, as people say nowadays. Why do they say that?"

"It's a film," Piers explained.

"Oh. Well, go softly for now, Trevor. Just put them in the picture and try to get some idea of their attitude. Exploratory discussions, the bureaucrats call it. Damn, I wish I could go myself."

"Best if I do it, I think," Hollowood said quickly. "I know the chap slightly. You should stay in the background until we get to a higher level in the Department."

"Do a bit of flag-waving," Roper advised. "Blame our problems on the competition with American capital."

Sir Trevor nodded abstractedly. His mind did not seem to be entirely on the matter at hand. Piers made up his mind to find out exactly what happened at the DTI.

"Let me give you some figures which may help you," he said. "I'll go and get them." He got up and left before Hollowood could decline the offer.

He walked quickly to his own office. There he picked up the latest sales statistics on the Capricorn and the English Diamond, and his economist's forecast of the effect of the English lorry on the Holmes rival. Then he unlocked the bottom drawer of his desk and took out what appeared to be an ordinary Bulldog clip. He fastened the papers together with the clip, and returned to Dean's office.

"Slip these in your briefcase in case you need them," he said to Hollowood. "What time is your appointment?"

"Two o'clock."

"I suppose we shouldn't keep you. Do you know the place to park near the DTI? I assume it's the Victoria Street building you're going to."

"It is, but I'm not driving," Hollowood said. He looked at his watch. "I ought to get started."

He nodded to Dean, and left. Roper followed.

He picked up his briefcase in his office, checked that his desk was locked, and went into his secretary's room.

"I may be out for the rest of the day," he told her.

"Can I say where you'll be?" she asked.

"No," he replied.

Piers stopped the Bentley in Park Lane three hours later. Ignoring the double yellow lines, he got out and walked slowly to the back of the car, stretching his legs. Hollowood had probably had a relaxed lunch on the train and was now feeling refreshed and eager, Piers reflected ruefully.

He opened the boot and took out a plain black peaked cap. He got back into the car, put the cap in the glove box, and drove on.

As he entered Victoria Street he put the cap on his head. In his dark suit, white shirt, and black tie, he now looked for all the world like a chauffeur.

He pulled in to the kerb at a news stand and held his hand out of the window. The vendor ran across to the car, took the proffered coins, and handed him an evening paper.

He drove on a hundred yards to the Government building and pulled into the tiny car park. It was full of cars, all Rolls-Royces and Bentleys. The chauffeurs stood around in the sunshine, leaning on the polished bonnets and smoking. Piers killed the engine.

A doorman looked at him then looked away again, assuming —as Piers intended—that he was just another chauffeur waiting for a VIP to emerge from the plate-glass doors.

Roper looked at his watch. Hollowood should arrive any minute. He opened the paper and held it up so that it concealed his face.

At a minute past two he folded the newspaper and set it down on the passenger seat. From the glove box he took a bakelite box about the size of a packet of cigarettes. An ear plug, attached to the box by a lead, made the whole thing look like a hearing aid. Piers pressed a switch on the side of the box, slotted the box into the bottom of his car stereo player, and put the plug in his ear.

He heard a hiss like radio static, and a muffled conversation which he could not quite make out. He cursed silently. The bundle of papers, with its microphone concealed in the Bulldog clip, must still be in Hollowood's briefcase.

Ten minutes later the sound suddenly became much louder. Piers winced and leaned forward to turn down the volume control on the receiver. He checked that the spools on the tape-deck were turning.

A lazy, cultured voice was saying: ". . . some idea of just how bad it is, Sir Trevor."

Hollowood's deeper, hesitant voice came through. "I have some figures on the effect of their activities on our performance." He began to read from Piers' documents.

He went on for a few minutes, then the civil servant interrupted. "I see the picture," the voice said, hesitating indolently over the glottal "c" in "picture". "But why are you telling me this?"

Hollowood took on an intimate, man-to-man tone. "I'd like an off-the-record reaction to what we plan to do about it. Strictly between the two of us."

"Of course."

"We have for some time been holding informal talks with a

major Japanese auto manufacturer on the possibility of a merger."

Piers clapped his hand to his ear involuntarily, pressing the plug in to hear more clearly. He held his breath.

"We have reached agreement on the broad outlines of the deal and quite a lot of the details," Hollowood went on. Piers listened in astonishment. "Basically, they will hold a substantial minority of the shares and have a say in the appointment of senior executives and directors."

"I suppose they want to reshuffle the management of the company," the civil servant put in.

"Yes. But the reconstituted management would have absolute control over everything but very general policy. In particular, we would have a veto on any decision involving redundancy."

There was a few moments' silence. Piers' mind spun with the sheer audacity of it all. Hollowood was conspiring behind his MD's back—it was a palace revolt. No doubt Hollowood was not alone. Some, if not all, of the pro-American bunch would be with him in the plot. And if they did not have a few Board members on their side, they must plan to win some over surreptitiously. Of course, it was not really a pro-American faction, but a pro-Japanese one.

Piers stopped speculating as the civil servant spoke again.

"Off the top of my head, I'd say the Government would have no objection to that. My Minister has already been embarrassed by the need to intervene in private enterprise."

"Excellent," Sir Trevor said. There was a scraping noise, then the conversation became unintelligible again. He had stuffed the papers back in his briefcase.

Piers took the plug out of his car and put the receiver back in the glove box. Then he started the Bentley and drove away. The doorman gave him a look of curiosity, but it was too late.

Piers headed for the Midlands.

Twenty-four hours later, on Friday afternoon, he was driving back to London again, with Anne by his side. It was the first time they had been alone since Piers had disgraced himself on her doorstep two days earlier. He would have preferred not to have given her a lift on this day—and he suspected she felt the same—but that would have caused comment in the office. You only have to be friends to give someone a lift, but you have to be lovers to quarrel, he thought.

They were both silent while he guided the car through the suburbs and out on to the motorway. The sloping hillsides on either side of the wide road were grey-green in the twilight. Piers was trying to formulate his apology, but he could not find a sentence which was both graceful and humble.

Finally he blurted out: "I behaved awfully on Wednesday night, and I wish I could find a way of saying I'm sorry."

"I thought it was cute," she said.

"God! A drunk rings the bell and makes you a graceless proposal of marriage, and you find it cute?"

"I know how much it takes to make you lose your poise. I was touched."

He stole a glance at her. She was watching him, and the look in her eyes said she felt sorry for him because he would never understand.

There was silence for a few miles. The countryside seemed to pass by very slowly, despite the speedometer. An evening breeze shepherded a flock of clouds into the fading sunlight, and Piers toyed with the idea of switching the car lights on. He made up his mind not to mention Wednesday night again.

"The builders start on the cottage next week," he said. His words fell awkwardly into the stillness inside the car.

"That was prompt," she said.

"I arranged it all before the contracts for the purchase were signed. I want to move in as quickly as possible." He added: "I'm rather fed up with hotel life," and instantly regretted the remark, for it recalled Wednesday.

"Will it take long?"

"A month or two for the alterations, and some weeks more for the decorating. I have some colour charts at home—will you help me choose furniture and so on?"

"You should hire an interior decorator," she replied. Piers winced at her tone. Perhaps she was not as blasé about his gauche proposal as she had pretended.

She read his mind. "It's not that I'm offended," she said. "But it's your house."

"I thought it might be ours," he said quietly.

"You really want to marry me," she said.

"Yes," he replied recklessly. That was two graceless proposals he had made. Now the time was wrong, the place was wrong, and he had half his mind on the road. But he pressed on grimly. "I am distraught. That was what Wednesday was all about. Long ago, I used to like my own company. Now I can do nothing but wish I was with you. I l-love you—oh, I wish I knew how to do this."

"Piers—" Her voice was oddly strained, and she stopped. When she spoke again she was coolly brutal.

"You have never learned to love, Piers, and now you're too old. You have discovered romance and you mistake it for the real thing. Love has nothing to do with desperate longing, or with the kind of aching passion we have. It's two people whose lives knit like pre-set gears. It gives contentment, not ecstasy."

"That's a very middle-aged attitude."

She went on as if he had not spoken. "You have learned too well to live alone. You're a cog that never locked with another. You're an emotional cripple, Piers. I would dearly love to teach you to walk, but I won't be your crutch."

Piers went white. "It sounds like an epitaph for an affair," he said.

"Perhaps it is. We should see less of each other."

"No!" he shouted. "Please, my darling. Don't say that. Let it go on—under whatever conditions, I don't mind."

135

"God, I hate myself when I realise what I've done to you."
She touched him lightly, running her fingernails along the
seam of his jacket. "I'm sorry, and I love you."

Quietly, not knowing whether he wanted her to hear it or
not, he said: "You don't know how badly I wanted you to say
that."

"You don't know how hard it was not to, all this time."

"Do you think . . . perhaps we might marry when I've
learned to walk, as you put it?" he asked with a small smile.

She took her hand away from him, and looked ahead out of
the windscreen. "You never will. Don't you know why you
fell in love with me?"

"It would take a long time—"

"No, you're wrong if you think that. It has nothing to do
with me, and everything to do with you."

"I don't believe you."

"You've read too many existentialist novels and not enough
women's magazines. Piers, you're in your forties. You look
back on your life and feel it has been rather worthless. You ask
yourself 'Why have I never known great love, changed the
world, risked my life for high principles?' Remember what you
said to me? 'I have done everything well and nothing good.'
It's called the male menopause."

"What does that matter, even if it's true? I love you, and
damn the reasons."

"But it won't last. That's why it matters. You will resign
yourself to being less than a hero. Mundane things like your
work and your finances will come to seem important again.
Reality throws a long shadow."

Out of the corner of his eye he could see her looking at his
face, waiting anxiously for his reaction. Eventually he said:
"Do you still want to know me, if you think all that?"

She turned away, looking out of the far window, concealing
her face from him. But he could hear the tears in her voice as
she whispered: "Damn you, yes, I do."

# Eight

When he got to work on Monday morning Roper telephoned
Anne's office.

"Did you have a good journey?" he asked her. They still
travelled back separately after their weekends at his flat.

"Yes—the train was singing the Verdi," she said.

"Listen. If we were to coincidentally both take a late lunch,
we might accidentally meet in the executive canteen at one
forty-five."

She laughed happily. It had been a good weekend. "All
right. But only once—twice would turn a coincidence into an
assignation."

"And that would be indecorous. Goodbye."

He hung up and began to plan the week. He decided to visit
the test track. That meant arranging it with Anthony Loughton, who could explain technicalities more concisely than anyone else in the Holmes Motor Corporation. On his way out he
picked up a memo to Loughton from his secretary's desk. "I'll
deliver this myself," he told her.

Loughton was behind his desk, with his jacket off and his
sleeves rolled up underneath expanding armlets, doodling on a
blueprint.

"Good weekend, Piers?" he asked pleasantly.

"Yes. I went to the opera."

"Ah. I love Verdi, do you?"

Piers was startled. "Verdi?" he said.

"That's the only one on, isn't it?"

"Oh, I wouldn't know. You weren't there, were you?"

"No such luck. I spent the weekend under the bonnet of a lorry."

Piers filed the exchange in his memory and changed the subject. "Will you be out at the track this week? I'd like to tag along if you will."

"How about Tuesday morning?"

"Fine." Piers left. A small frown wrinkled between his eyebrows as he walked down the corridor to his own office. Loughton had not struck him as the type to be so fond of opera that he knew every London performance even when he was out of town.

He sat at his desk, reflecting. He lit a cigarette and savoured the chemical kick. A frightening possibility crossed his mind. He put the cigarette carefully in a wide glass ashtray and picked up his phone.

"Yes, sir?" his secretary said.

"Outside line," he told her. When he heard the dialling tone he rang the number of his London flat. There was no reply—his cleaning lady would not be there yet.

He put the receiver on the desk in front of him and unscrewed the mouthpiece. Taped to the inside was a small disc about the size of a florin.

So Anthony Loughton was bugging Piers' phone.

Without touching the device, he replaced the mouthpiece and cradled the handset. A pattern was emerging.

His cigarette was a long worm of ash with a millimetre of tobacco left. He brushed it over the ashtray's grooved edge into the bowl, then wiped his fingers with a paper tissue. He got up and walked to the Public Relations Department.

Hudson stood up as he entered, but Piers waved the young man to his seat. "I know my way," he said. He crossed the room to the tiny office where the press cuttings were filed.

He located the personnel scrapbooks, took the top one, and laid it on a table. He drew up the one chair in the room and began to go back in time through the file. After a while he lit a cigarette, ignoring the notices which said "No smoking" in large red capitals.

The cuttings he wanted began to turn up after he had ploughed through a year and a half. Most of them were from the trade press and house publications, although there was one in a local newspaper.

They recorded a round-the-world trip Loughton had made to boost Holmes' export drive. He had visited car dealers, talked on radio, met importers and attended functions. There were pictures of him smiling, shaking hands, getting on aeroplanes, and looking at bits of paper.

He had spent a fortnight in Japan.

Roper replaced the heavy book in its stack and returned to his office. He had to establish one more link in the chain.

He rang Anne. "I shan't be coming to town this weekend," he said. "I have to visit the cottage and talk to the builders, and there's a lot of work at the office I must clear. I'm sorry."

"So am I," she said softly.

He sighed as she hung up. It was the first lie he had ever told her.

Then he rang a local number and hired a small car.

Anthony Loughton's Jaguar shot out of the executive car park and joined the queue of vehicles waiting to pass through the works gate. Two more cars queued behind him. In the staff car park on the opposite side of the queue, Roper started the cheap family saloon and moved forward.

A third car had joined the queue by the time Piers got there. The guards had decided to hold a security check, and were stopping occasional vehicles to look in the boots.

By the time Loughton got to the gate, they were bored with the idea, and waved the Jaguar and the four cars behind it through the gate. They all turned left on to the road into the town.

They drove fast along the dual carriageway through the

industrial area, then slowed to a crawl as they reached the town and hit the Friday night rush hour. Piers stayed close to Loughton's Jaguar, watching his indicator lights. The sunshade of the saloon was pulled down, throwing a shadow over Piers' face. The car was a popular shade of bronze, and very forgettable.

Loughton took a right fork on the far side of the town, confirming Roper's expectation that the man was going home. As they approached the select suburb where he lived, Piers let him get just out of sight and stayed a corner behind.

The saloon turned into Loughton's street just in time to see the brake lights of the Jaguar blink into a drive. The large detached houses stood well back from the road along one side. Opposite was a triangular village green, dotted with trees. Piers drove past the house and around the green.

Opposite Loughton's house was a small pub with a large yard. Trees in the garden of the next-door house overhung the yard fence. Piers reversed under the trees and killed the engine. He clambered into the back seat of the car and settled in a corner. As the evening dimmed into night he would become invisible.

At nine o'clock on Saturday morning Piers yawned and resisted the temptation to scratch at the stubble on his cheeks. No one had gone in or out of the house all night. He took two amphetamine pills from his waistcoat pocket and forced them down his dry throat. He was getting too old for this sort of work.

At half-past nine the front door of Loughton's house opened. Piers picked up the binoculars from the seat beside him and put them to his eyes. He saw Loughton, dressed in slacks and a knitted cardigan, walk over to the double garage and go in.

Minutes later the Jaguar pulled out of the drive. Piers started the engine of the saloon. When the Jaguar turned the corner he followed it.

He had to take greater risks now, because he had no idea where Loughton was going. Early shopping traffic gave him a little cover, but when they got out to an open country road he had to tag along a hundred yards behind and hope Loughton was not in an observant frame of mind.

Fortunately the journey was short. The Jaguar pulled into the entrance of a golf club, and Piers drove on past.

He stopped on the brow of a hill a quarter of a mile further along, and surveyed the geography. The golf course was in a dip between two low hills. Most of the course was visible from a spot just off the road, where the hill he had stopped on was highest. He drove on to a lay-by and parked.

He took his binoculars and a camera with a telephoto lens and walked back up the hill. At the top he crossed a ditch and a fence and entered a wood. When he had found his vantage point he selected a tall tree.

Slinging his equipment around his neck, he shinned up the tree, ignoring the damage to his £100 suit. He made himself comfortable on a branch half way up and lifted the binoculars.

He located Loughton, putting at the first hole already. The deputy MD appeared to play well. Piers followed his movement around the course. He was playing alone. From time to time he dropped out of sight behind a rise.

At the fifth hole Piers was astonished to see Loughton pick up his ball at the edge of the green and move on to the next hole. He appeared to be hurrying.

He teed off on the sixth. A couple of players who had just finished that hole watched his ball land and waited for him to catch them up. That was odd—they should have pressed on in order to get out of Loughton's way.

Piers took a closer look at the two other men as Loughton walked up to the green. Suddenly his memory clicked. He picked up the camera and aimed it.

Through the telephoto lens he watched Loughton smile and shake hands with the men. Loughton put his hand into his

141

cardigan pocket and brought out a small piece of paper. He handed it to the man who had rung a bell in Piers' memory. As the paper passed from one hand to another, Piers pressed the shutter.

The two men walked away and Loughton resumed his game. Piers scrambled down from the tree and returned to his car.

He drove into the town, left the car at the hirer's, and walked to his hotel. He ordered a meal of rare steak and fried eggs to be brought to his room. He bathed, shaved, and put on a dressing-gown.

When he had eaten the meal he lay on the bed. He went to sleep wondering what to do.

Roper looked at Lord Shipley's house through the binoculars. Most of the lights were now out. Piers knew that Shipley always stayed up late, reading, after his household went to bed. It was now 11 o'clock. Piers started the Bentley.

An unmade road led up to the house, with no clear sign of when the common ended and the grounds began. It was a three-storey building, and its symmetrical rows of arched windows gave it a dolls' house appearance. Piers stopped the car on the tarmacadamed courtyard and rang the bell.

The butler answered the door in his shirtsleeves.

"My name is Piers Roper. Would you give Lord Shipley my apologies for calling so late?"

The butler appraised Piers with a perceptive glance and replied: "I'm sure he will see you, sir. Would you follow me?"

Roper's shoes clattered on the highly polished wood floor as he crossed the hall. Shipley got up as he walked into the room.

"My dear chap! I hope you don't bring bad news."

"I do, but not the life-or-death kind," Piers replied.

"Sit down," the Chairman said, pointing to a wide floral arm-chair. "Drink?"

"Scotch." Piers sat down, putting his briefcase beside the

chair. "I have a story to tell you. It won't take long, but it may be hard to believe."

Shipley put the decanter and water jug on an antique occasional table in front of Piers. He lifted the lid of a cigarette box and put that beside the whisky.

"Well," he said, settling back in his own chair, "it must be quite a tale that brings you here at this time of night."

"I wanted to see you alone, without anyone else knowing about it. You will understand why I'm being so furtive." He leaned forward and measured water into his glass.

"Make yourself comfortable, and then tell."

"A couple of months ago, I bought a picture—a Derain. I discovered quite by accident that it had belonged to Sir Trevor Hollowood. I made some more inquiries, and found out that he had sold about half a million pounds' worth of paintings during the last year or so."

Shipley raised his eyebrows over the rims of his glasses. Piers went on: "I was curious, for reasons I won't go into, to know why Sir Trevor should do that. I warn you this story gets much more unsavoury as I go along.

"It turns out that he was involved in some unethical share dealing over a company called Selectronics, which he thought Holmes would buy up. He caught a very nasty cold over that. This part of the story can easily be checked, you realise."

Shipley's voice was expressionless. "Yes," he said.

"I let it be known that I realised he had sold his art collection. Two things then happened which made me seriously suspicious. The first was an attempt to obtain material with which to blackmail me. The second was the discovery that Sir Trevor had so managed the finances of the company that we may be forced to merge with another motor manufacturer.

"I was fairly certain then that he had in some way betrayed his colleagues. Next, I found out how.

"He is party to a conspiracy to overthrow the current management of Holmes during a takeover by a Japanese company.

"I believe the deal was negotiated by Anthony Loughton during his visit to Japan. I first had doubts about his integrity when I discovered he had bugged my telephone. I later confirmed them.

"Loughton has been selling company secrets to English Motors, in order to bring Holmes to its knees. That explains why they have done so well against us in both cars and commercial vehicles for the past six months.

"Meanwhile Sir Trevor was mismanaging our finances. I doubt whether he was a willing party to the plot—I imagine Loughton found out about his Stock Market indiscretions, and used that knowledge as a lever.

"Any time now there will be a takeover bid by the Japanese company. Some members of the board are probably being lobbied already. And I don't doubt that a condition of the Japanese offer will be that Loughton becomes MD."

Piers finished and waited for Shipley's reaction. He said: "You were right that your story would be hard to believe."

Piers opened his briefcase. He took out a photograph and passed it to Shipley. "The man to whom Loughton is passing that piece of paper is Michael Lennon, one of Britain's top industrial spies. I imagine you will be able to confirm that."

Next he took from the case a portable cassette player.

"I would prefer that you did not ask me how this recording came into my possession," he said. He pressed a button. Shipley tilted his head on one side as Sir Trevor's voice, and that of the DTI civil servant, emerged through the static.

When the tape ended there was a long silence. Piers helped himself to more whisky, and lit a cigarette.

Eventually Shipley shook his grey head slowly from side to side. "You realise the choice I am faced with," he said quietly. "Either you or Sir Trevor is lying." He sighed softly. "This is the way business is done these days. I think it's sad."

"I don't think you're forced to decide whether to believe

me," Piers said.

Lord Shipley raised his eyes to Roper's face.

Piers continued: "If what I've said is right, there is only one way you can retain control of Holmes. That is to arrange a merger with another company. If I am wrong, you can simply call it off when no Japanese offer arrives."

"And if you are right, we will still have a battle on our hands."

"I think we would win it."

"I'm not sure I want to fight it."

Shipley stood up and walked over to a corner. For the first time Piers noticed an old Labrador asleep on a rug. Shipley bent down and stroked its head. The dog opened one eye, looked at its master, and went back to sleep.

"I'm an engineer, you know," Shipley said meditatively. "I designed Holmes' first post-war car. It wasn't as good as it should have been, because of the way we ran our production lines. A few years later they put me in charge of the factories."

Piers thought he might as well have been talking about an amateur dramatic society, the easy way he spoke of promotion within a major industry. But any comment would have almost been an invasion of privacy.

"When I got there, I realised the factories were hamstrung by the way the company's finances were run. Later on they put me in charge of that. By then it seemed to me that the lead from top management and the board was at fault. When I got to that level I became very dissatisfied with the work of our designers. I should have stayed at the drawing-board. I would have been frustrated, but not disillusioned."

He sat down again, and poured whisky. Instead of drinking it, he gazed into the glass, seeing the past there.

Finally he put it down untouched and stood up. "I'm sure you don't want to sit here and listen to an old man's regrets," he said. "Thank you for coming here—and for your vigilance. I'll fly to Detroit tomorrow."

He saw Piers to the door. They shook hands and said good night.

"It's beautiful," Anne said.

Piers walked into the centre of the drawing-room of the converted cottage. A coal fire made cheerful noises in the grate, despite the mildness of the late summer evening. The deep-pile carpet was a warm shade of ivory, blending with the faintly-patterned wallpaper. A few antiques furnished the room, placed carefully to conceal the new radiators under the windows. The low beams of the ceiling had been revarnished, and the smell was still just detectable in the air.

They walked back through the hall into the kitchen. It was large and light, with fitted wall cupboards and shining new cooker, fridge, sink unit and gas boiler. A Welsh dresser of light wood up against one wall was filled with utensils, and on the worktop were a toaster, an electric kettle, and a food mixer. In the middle of the room was a long table.

The second of the two cottages was given over to the dining-room and bedrooms. Anne gave a delighted gasp at the very expensive paintings on the dining-room walls.

The master bedroom was Roper's *pièce de résistance*. An enormous divan covered with a duvet dominated the room. It was half as big again as an ordinary double bed. The flowered duvet cover matched the soft rose pink of the walls. The ceiling above the bed was one huge mirror. Elegant white wardrobes stretched all along one wall. There were two dressing-tables: one square and chunky, the other daintily feminine.

Anne sat on the bed. "This is a bedroom for two," she said unsmilingly.

Piers sat beside her and took her hand. "I haven't given up hope that you will live here as my wife," he said. He paused, to allow her to stop him if she wanted to. She said nothing.

Piers went on: "You were right when you said I never knew what love was. I do now, you know. This house isn't a love

146

nest. It's a place for people to *live*—for two people to share their lives. I have never met anyone I wanted to do that with —and I don't suppose I shall again, if I lose you. You're not a whim, or a male menopause. You're the only person in the world who fits me like a—well, I don't know. A jigsaw puzzle." He looked down at her hand in his. "Do you know how unused I am to begging for something?"

"I know. Piers, I love you. When I met you I thought you were a pompous ass. I seduced you out of curiosity, and I fell in love with the man under the façade. I wish I knew how you would feel towards a wife."

"Will you gamble on me?"

"I don't know. Don't push it, Piers. I can't tell what's going on inside me any more. I think—I think I want to gamble on you. I don't know."

He squeezed her hand. "I couldn't ask you to say more."

She became matter-of-fact. "You realise one of us would have to leave Holmes."

"Yes . . ."

"And you were assuming it would be me."

"I suppose I—"

"You see, Piers, I know you too well." She shook her head in frustration. "That's just the kind of clash that could have us hating each other. Why shouldn't it be you who leaves?"

Piers wanted desperately to say Yes, I'll leave Holmes. But he couldn't—not now, of all times. He could not duck out in the middle of a crisis, leaving Loughton and Hollowood to gloat over their victory.

"There isn't any reason you would know about," he told her. "Although you must have heard rumours about what's going on. Anyway, the problem may solve itself before long."

"Go on."

"Well, two foreign companies have made bids for a large chunk of Holmes. There's a behind-the-scenes battle between two factions of executives over who will win. Either way, there will be management changes. It's quite likely that one of us will be out of a job by the time it's over."

She touched his cheek. "You shouldn't really tell me that sort of thing, should you."

"These days I do an awful lot of things which horrify my instincts."

She put her hand inside his jacket and undid a shirt button. He felt her nails on the skin of his belly. She gave her rich, fruity chuckle. "Do something horrifying to me now," she said.

He pushed her backwards on to the bed and kissed her.


The evening before the crucial board meeting, Roper paid a visit to the home of Sir Trevor Hollowood.

The battle was out in the open now, with artillery lined up and trenches dug. The voting intentions of a few board members were known, but there were sufficient waverers to keep the result in doubt.

The Japanese offer was, inevitably, slightly better, as the American one had been negotiated from a position of weakness. But the authority of Lord Shipley, which counted for a lot on the board, compensated for that.

Roper had to go to the board meeting, to present the case for the Americans. Loughton would be there, with Hollowood as his second, to argue for the Japanese.

Roper parked behind Sir Trevor's Holmes Diplomat and knocked on the front door. The financial director opened the door himself. He wore carpet slippers and was smoking a pipe.

He looked at Roper for a moment and said: "I suppose you'd better come in."

Piers followed him into a modern sitting-room furnished with chrome, glass, and black leather upholstery. He sat down uninvited.

"I shan't beat about the bush," he said. "I want to make you an offer. My side of the bargain would be that I give you a tape recording, which I have in my pocket; and my word that

I can ensure that Anthony Loughton will never reveal what he knows about your dealings in Selectronics shares."

Hollowood took his pipe out of his mouth and nodded. "I can guess what my side of the bargain is," he said sadly.

"Gentlemen," began Lord Shipley. "You all know why Mr. Loughton and Mr. Roper are here today. However, it is customary to ask the board's assent to the presence of non-members. Can I take it I have your permission?"

He paused for objections, then went on: "We have to consider two proposals for merging the Holmes Motor Corporation with foreign companies. Mr. Loughton will give us the details of the offer from Hotawa, then Mr. Roper will tell us about the one from Greatlakes Motors. Finally we will have to decide which one to recommend to our shareholders."

Down the table, a director known to favour the Japanese interrupted: "I notice Sir Trevor has not arrived."

"I expect he has been delayed, Mr. Masterson," Shipley said. "However he is, as a full-time working director, familiar with what Mr. Loughton and Mr. Roper are going to tell us. I propose we start without him."

Loughton began to speak. Piers listened to the first few sentences, but the line was all too predictable. In his mind he ran over the personal consequences to himself if he should lose this afternoon. He would certainly have to resign from Holmes, but that was secondary. He would have failed Palmer for the first time ever. Michael Lennon's firm would gain the ascendancy over Palmer's operation. The blow to morale could be fatal.

Whereas, if Piers won, he would be almost certain to become Managing Director of the new Holmes. That would mean close liaison with the American partners, and consequent access to their secrets. Piers would become the most valuable industrial spy in the world. The designs, marketing plans and research results of a major US motor manufacturer were worth literally millions.

Loughton spoke for almost an hour. Roper took half that time, knowing that the directors would be getting sore backsides by now. Each of them had a fat file of reports and figures pertaining to each offer, so it was only necessary to give them a direction through the mass of facts.

When Piers had finished, Mr. Masterson stood up. He said: "I cannot understand why Sir Trevor is not here. I know that he intended to bring with him his own personal report on the decision facing this board. However, I do have a draft of that report, and I think the board should know that he strongly favoured the Japanese offer."

Lord Shipley shot a worried look at Piers. Another director chipped in. Any time now would do, Piers thought. He glanced at his watch. The boardroom door opened.

A uniformed messenger came in and silently handed an envelope to Lord Shipley. With his eyes on the director who was speaking, Shipley tore open the envelope. Piers saw him glance at it, and watched his eyes widen in surprise.

The director finished: ". . . must agree with Sir Trevor, the Japanese bid is financially superior."

"Gentlemen," Shipley said. "I have just received a letter from Sir Trevor which I think I ought to read to you. It reads: 'Dear Shipley. I deeply regret that it is at a time like this that I must tender my resignation from the Board of Directors of the Holmes Motor Corporation. You will know that I intended to advise the Board to accept the Japanese offer I now realise that I was totally mistaken. But this is not my sole reason for resigning. Looking back over the past two years, I feel that the financial advice which I have given the company has been seriously at fault too often.'

"The rest of the letter is of a more informal nature," Shipley said. "I won't read it aloud, but I will pass it around the table." He handed it to Loughton, who sat on his immediate left.

Loughton's face was deep red. He looked at the single sheet of paper for a few moments, passed it on, and stood up.

"Excuse me a moment, sir," he said to Shipley. He walked out. Piers raised an eyebrow at the Chairman, who nodded. Piers followed Loughton out.

He caught up with him in the ante-room. "Loughton!" he called.

"Well?"

Piers took a photograph from his pocket. It was the one he had shown Lord Shipley six weeks before.

"You can keep that, Loughton. Sir Trevor has the negative." He lowered his voice. "If word ever gets out about Hollowood's indiscretion over Selectronics shares, I fancy your connection with Mr. Lennon will also become public knowledge."

Loughton paled. He took the photograph, tore it in two with a savage jerk of his wrists, and stuffed the halves into his inside pocket.

His anger evaporated, and something inside him seemed to acknowledge defeat. "I didn't do it for the money, you know," he said. "There had to be a change of government at Holmes —Dean had to go. He's a sick man, and he won't admit it. All I did was to hurry things up. Really, that's all."

He was a pathetic sight: the loser making excuses. Piers wavered between pity and contempt, then banished both from his mind. The important thing now was to say something which would stick in Loughton's mind, so that later, when the man started to wonder just how Piers had got hold of the incriminating photograph, his suspicion would be allayed.

"There is no excuse for disloyalty," Piers said, and turned on his heel. As he entered the boardroom and took his seat, he thought how much Anne would despise the hypocrisy of that remark.

Piers sat and studied his new boss. Harry Heston was overweight and wore a ginger hairpiece, but Piers was determined not to dislike him for it.

Heston was playing the role of the tough-minded American sweeping the cobwebs out of a fuddy-duddy English company. What he lacked in ideas he was trying to make up in abrasiveness. Piers adopted the line of least resistance. Heston did not know the company well enough to insist upon major policy swerves at a few days' notice: he could do little damage.

The American pointed a manicured finger at a page in a file. "What the hell is this leather upholstery plant doing here?" he asked.

"It's an option on the most expensive Diplomats," Piers replied.

"It do much business?"

"Very little."

"So I say again: What the hell's it doing here?"

"It's a prestige thing. In theory, the Diplomat competes with luxury cars like Mercedes and Jaguar. Most of our customers decide to save their money, but they like to think it's the kind of car which can have leather seats. In addition, we use the better upholstery in our advertising."

"Scrap it," said Heston.

Piers said nothing. On its own, the decision was a bad one. But Piers had plans to scrap the Diplomat altogether. At present the luxury ranges produced by both Holmes and English were making very small profits. Roper planned to leave that field to English. It was a move which would serve both of his employers. But Piers did not mention it to Heston. If he did, Heston would take the idea up, insist upon it, and present it to his superiors as his own idea.

"Okay." Heston took Piers' silence for assent, and closed the file with a bang. "Now tell me something: why have you got a Personnel Department?"

"It handles the welfare programme and provides a back-up service to operating departments on matters like hiring and firing, redundancy, and labour relations."

"What would happen if you scrapped it?"

"The whole department?" Roper raised a sceptical eyebrow, but the gesture was wasted on Heston. "Its work would be done by the operational departments."

"Right." Heston let his fist fall on the desk with a thump, and Piers almost laughed at the cliché. "And done a lot faster too, because they've all got more important things to get on with. See my point?"

"Certainly."

"But don't agree with it, eh?"

"It would be a worthwhile experiment."

"Then we'll do it." He picked up a sheet of paper and tossed it across the desk. "We'll decimate the department. I suggest these redundancies."

Piers saw with a guilty start that Anne was to be fired. "Why leave anybody at all?" he said.

"To run welfare services, which is all that is really their concern. Besides, I don't want line management worrying about cricket pitches and social clubs."

"Fine," said Piers.


Piers rolled off Anne and lay on his back on the pink sheet, looking at the low cottage ceiling. He reached for a tissue and wiped the sweat from his belly, then got up on one elbow and brushed the paper handkerchief over Anne's breasts.

He got his breathing under control and said: "My darling, you are more than any man has the right to ask for." He dipped his head and kissed the skin of her shoulder. Her body was flushed with exertion.

She opened her eyes and looked at him. Her voice was low and lazy. "And you are a very beautiful man," she said. "Would you kiss me again, just a little?"

He kissed her lips then rested his head on the pillow, studying her profile. Slowly the heady euphoria was replaced by a seductive sleepiness.

After a while she said: "And a victorious man, too."

"Mmmm," he said, and stretched. Now the sleepiness drifted away, and his body tingled with new energy.

"Does it make you happy—the victory?" she asked.

"Nope," he said.

"Nope? Where on earth did you pick up that expression?"

"Sorry. It's Henry Heston. He talks like a character out of 'Gunfight At The O.K. Corral'. Must be infectious. But the victory doesn't make me happy."

"Why not?"

"Now that I've got it I see that it doesn't matter much. What I really want is you: you living here with me, you with me every day at breakfast, you playing my records and helping me buy clothes, you as my full-time, publicly acknowledged life partner."

She rolled over and leaned on his chest, fingering the bristles below his Adam's apple. "I know," she said softly. "But what shall we do about the ubiquitous Holmes Motor Corporation?"

He looked at her chin. "Henry Heston has solved that problem," he said.

Some of the colour drained from her face, and her mouth hardened into a straight line. "What is that supposed to mean?"

"He's disbanding the Personnel Department. He thinks we can do without it, and he's probably right. Anyway, just now I can't quarrel with him over things like that. So I agreed. Your job is one of the ones which goes."

She got off the bed and crossed the room for cigarettes. She opened the packet, put one in her mouth, and raised the lighter. "Just like that," she said. She flicked the wheel and held the flame to the cigarette.

Piers sat up and spread his hands, palms upwards, in a gesture of helplessness. "I couldn't do anything about it, and it's what we wanted. One of us had to leave Holmes."

"Fine." She blew out a long stream of smoke. "'You've got no job now, Anne darling, so how about marrying me'. Christ, I've had some proposals but that beats the lot." She gave a short laugh.

Piers' face wrinkled in pained puzzlement. "I don't understand you," he said.

"Then just think about it! I'm made redundant—therefore Holmes has decided it can do without me. The stigma will always be there. I had a career, Piers, and you've just cleverly put a stop to it in your own selfish interest."

He strode across to her and took hold of her arm. "Darling—"

"Romanticism is not your strong point, remember?" She turned away from him and he dropped his hands.

"You'll get another job. I can—"

"You fool!" she blazed. "I don't just want a job, I want a career. It has something to do with my self-respect. And I don't want a job that you find for me either."

"My God." Piers dropped his arms and let his shoulders slump. A note of anger crept into his voice. "Why is it always me who has to prove his love? Why do you ask so much of me? Do you think I should have left Holmes?"

"Yes!" She turned to face him again, and he was shocked to see that she was crying. "Don't you see. Piers? You told me you had changed—you were no longer a one-track man. I wanted to believe you." Her voice cracked in a sob. "I wanted to. So I forced you to choose between Holmes and me—and you chose Holmes, you stupid, stupid bastard."

"But you don't understand the whole thing." Piers wanted desperately to tell her now: about Palmer, about English Motors, about electronic bugs and telephoto lenses and all-night stakeouts. But a lifetime of secrecy and self-discipline had built a wall in his mind, and he could not get the words out.

"I do understand," she was saying. "I understand too well." She paused. "Would you leave Holmes now?"

He stared at her for a long moment. "No," he said finally.
"Then there's nothing more to be said, is there." She picked
up her bra from the floor and began to put it on.

Piers could not bear to watch her. He wanted to say something, to continue the quarrel, to make her stay with him a
little longer. But he could think of nothing to tell her.

He turned away and walked blindly through the house to
the back door. The cool air on his naked body made him
shiver, but he did not realise it. He walked into the garden and
stood looking at the bark of an apple tree, struggling with his
mental paralysis. He slowly drew back his fist and punched
the tree savagely. Then he clutched the broken hand in his
armpit and groaned with the pain.

The beach was as wet and bleak as it had been a year ago. The
rain beat tirelessly down on the oblivious waves, the raindrops
making tiny ripples within the larger pattern. Nothing had
changed down here among these rocks.

Piers looked at the bowler-hatted man by his side. He no
longer felt any reverence for the powerful mind and body of
Palmer. He was just another factor to be dealt with in a
mechanical life.

"Dean and Loughton's resignations will be officially announced next week," Piers said flatly. "I become Managing
Director, Shipley stays as Chairman."

Palmer gave a rare smile. "This is the kind of coup I always
knew you would bring off one day," he said. "Needless to say,
the possibilities for opening up in America are quite staggering.
I want you to build our American operation, Piers."

Roper nodded wordlessly.

"You can spend a few years at it, and we shall both become
millionaires." He paused, and Piers suddenly sensed tension in
the set of Palmer's shoulders. The man went on: "Then I shall
retire, Piers, and you will take over."

Roper let the news sink in. A spark of enthusiasm lit inside him as he began to see what that would mean. His thoughts leapt ahead to the changes he would make in the organisation Palmer had built—some new companies to confuse inquiring minds, a more powerful support system for individual field operatives, some—

Then he remembered Anne, and the picture dimmed.

"Yes, I shall," he said flatly.

"Well, I'm going to push off out of the rain," Palmer said. He shook Piers' hand. "An absolutely splendid result all around," he said. He took a step across the pebbles, then changed his mind and came back.

"Not much is hidden from me, Piers," he said.

Roper wondered whether he could possibly be talking about Anne, then realised that he must mean that.

Palmer sighed. "The wound will heal, you know," he said. He seemed to contemplate saying something else, then turned around abruptly and walked away.

The wound will heal: the words reverberated in Piers' mind like a tune which one cannot get out of one's head. He lit a cigarette and stared into the perpetual motion of the waves. A splendid result all around, he thought.

He smoked the cigarette down to the butt and lit another. His mouth tasted scorched, but he pulled the hot smoke into his lungs with fierce determination. The cigarette fell from his fingers and blew across the pebbles in the wind. There was a faint fizz as it settled into a puddle and was doused. The wound will heal, he said to himself.

His face creased in an expression of pain. He sank slowly to the ground, his knees dipping into the shallow edge of the sea. The wound will heal. He composed his face and looked out across the ocean, calm now.

"But there will always be a small scar," he said aloud. The sound was whipped away by the breeze and scattered in the air like so much pathetic flotsam.

# THE TEARS OF AUTUMN

## CHARLES McCARRY

On November 1st 1963 the President of South Vietnam and his brother were murdered. Just three weeks later there followed an act of traditional Vietnamese vengeance which shook the world—the assassination of President John Kennedy.

With this remarkable chain of events Charles McCarry, the author of THE MIERNIK DOSSIER, begins his new novel, a book which has placed him in the front rank of the great spy thriller writers. And in the character of Paul Christopher he has created a superb portrait of the good intelligence agent and the seedy half-world he inhabits. THE TEARS OF AUTUMN is a magnificent novel, truthful, finely crafted and compulsively readable.

'Ranks him up there with Le Carré in a select class of two'
*Daily Mail*

**CORONET BOOKS**

## MORE FICTION FROM CORONET BOOKS